The Spirit Window

The Spirit Window

JOYCE SWEENEY

Delacorte Press

Published by
Delacorte Press
Bantam Doubleday Dell Publishing Group, Inc.
1540 Broadway
New York, New York 10036

Copyright © 1998 by Joyce Sweeney

Library of Congress Cataloging-in-Publication Data

Sweeney, Joyce.
    The spirit window / Joyce Sweeney.
        p.   cm.
    Summary: A trip to Florida that is meant to heal the rift between her father and her grandmother forces both fifteen-year-old Miranda and her father to face feelings they have long suppressed.
    ISBN 0-385-32510-X
    [1. Parent and child—Fiction.   2. Grandmothers—Fiction.
3. Death—Fiction.   4. Florida—Fiction.]   I. Title.
PZ7.S97427Sp   1998
[Fic]—dc21   97-15345
                                                                                      CIP
                                                                                      AC

The text of this book is set in 13-point Adobe Granjon.
Book design by Susan Clark

Manufactured in the United States of America
April 1998
10 9 8 7 6 5 4 3 2 1
BVG

To the Thursday Group

Heidi Boehringer, Dennis Bailey, Dorian Cirrone, Daniel Deluca, Marci Finklestein, Niki Fotopoulos, Nancy Greenberg, Christian Henz, Nancy Knutson, Joan Lankford, Chauncey Mabe, Mary Mastin, Joan Mazza, Joan McIver, Stuart McIver, Lynda Patten, Mark Peres, Carla Pittman, Bill Rea, Gloria Rothstein, Lucille Shulklapper, Mark Smith and Noreen Wald

Thank you all for support, inspiration and friendship.

Acknowledgments

Thanks to Jay, Heidi and Joan for feedback, to George Nicholson for validation, and to Michelle Poploff for insight.

one

"A few more miles and we'll be off the turnpike. That's when you'll start to see the real Florida!"

Miranda, sprawled on the backseat, didn't even bother to look. For the first eight hours they'd been in Florida, she had dutifully checked the view every time her father made an optimistic remark. It had always been the same—scruffy pine trees and gathering storm clouds. Once, a huge, careening bird that looked exactly like a vulture. This was the real Florida. The postcards were a lie.

"I think I can smell the ocean," he continued.

"Honey, shut up. Everyone's tired." This was Ariel's voice. Miranda was surprised. Her stepmother had been asleep since Ocala, when the factory outlet billboards started to dwindle. The wind had sucked a skein of Ariel's bright gold hair out the window. It whipped the side of the car as if it wanted back in. *Extreme despair,* Miranda thought, *when Ariel doesn't care what her hair is doing.*

"Now!" her father cried, like a magician reaching into a hat.

Miranda sat up. They were exiting the Florida Turnpike. The road ahead was framed by flashing tollbooths. She wound the strap of her Nikon around her hand, in case the splendors of the "real Florida" were about to explode in front of them.

The toll collector was a young man with a pink tank top and twenty-inch dreadlocks. Miranda slid to the left, trying to pull him into focus. He was the most interesting sight since Georgia. Happily, her father was creating a distraction.

"We're from Cincinnati," he chirped, offering a folded ten-dollar bill. "And we can't get over your beautiful weather!"

The young man actually flinched. "*My* weather!" he said. A starburst of lines crossed his forehead. Miranda shot the picture. With any luck, she had caught the toll collector's frown and her father's fading smile. "In like ten minutes, it's going to rain cats!" He counted out their change.

Miranda's father struggled to communicate. "I meant the warmth. It's so warm."

The toll collector made a little three-fingered sweep, a gesture between a salute and a push. "People waiting behind you, sir."

They entered the real Florida. A two-lane road bordered by the same scraggly pine trees. Miranda took a picture she could use later in life when she confronted her father with all his mistakes. He had told Miranda he encouraged his patients to sit down with their parents and go over all the grievances of childhood. It sounded like a great idea.

Ariel, meanwhile, had reached a cranky overload. "Do you have to make a fool of yourself everywhere you go, Richard?"

He turned a half-profile toward his young wife. Miranda thought he looked handsome and fired off a shot, hoping the overcast light would halo his face. "I don't think I made a fool of myself," he said. "Miranda? Did I make a fool of myself?"

Before Miranda could answer, Ariel went on. "We're in south Florida now, Rich. That guy could have been a Jamaican terrorist with a gun."

Jamaican terrorist? Miranda thought. It would take too much energy to discuss it, though. Instead, she took Ariel's picture. Ariel looked interesting when she was angry. Like an angel spitting or a marble statue flipping the bird.

"Hey! Cut it out! My hair is all over the place."

"It looks sexy," Miranda's father said.

Ariel finger-combed her hair, shaping it into a horse-tail, which she began to braid. "Close up the car, Richard," she grumbled. "In a minute, it's going to rain cats!"

"How far are we from Grandma's?" Miranda asked over the whine of the car sealing itself. "Why don't we stop and eat something? I feel like we've been in this car all our lives."

"No, no, we're practically there! Ari, look at the map. I think we're just on this road for a few minutes, then A1A to the causeway, and boom, we're on Turtle Island."

Miranda slumped in her seat. She was trapped in a children's book. *Raining Cats on Turtle Island.* She thought of all the things she could be doing right now if she were back in Cincinnati. Cruising the malls with her best friend, Ginger, swimming, taking a summer photography clinic. Miranda didn't even know where she would get chemicals here. Turtle Island probably had a nice little Eckerd's or something where ladies like her grandmother had pictures of their cats developed.

"Why are we in this forest, Rich?" Ariel pried open a

bobby pin with her teeth and speared her braid, securing it against the nape of her neck. "Where am I going to go shopping in this hellhole?"

Richard suddenly raised his voice. "Look! My mother could be dying, all right? We're going here because my mother has refused to speak to me most of my adult life and now she's apparently willing to, and I thought, what the heck, it might be good to try and make peace with my only living parent—excuse me—my only living relative before she leaves this world. How selfish of me! If this is too much of a nuisance to you, we'll turn the car around and go on a really fun vacation!"

Ariel went stiff during this speech, but Miranda felt strangely excited. Her father rarely lost control, but when he did, he seemed more alive. She wanted to take a picture of him, his shoulders stiff with anger, his blue eyes blazing a challenge to Ariel . . . but of course she couldn't.

Ariel turned from him to face the greenish black sky ahead. "Oh, I guess I'm some kind of unsupportive bitch," she said.

Already back to professionalism, he appeared to count a few beats before murmuring, "I didn't say that, Ari."

Ariel looked sideways at him—a beautiful, surly child.

Richard smiled—a warm, forgiving father.

Where am I in all this? Miranda wondered. *Oh, yes, the photographer.* She focused on the stormy sky between them, and the Nikon let out a defiant whir.

Both of them turned on her. The car swerved as a skeleton of lightning tore through the blackness in the east. "Shit!" Richard faced the road again.

Thunder exploded.

"Shit!" Ariel shrieked.

Miranda began firing shots, hoping to catch the lightning. *Whir, whir, flash, crack, whir.*

"Pull over!" Ariel said. "I'm freaking out!"

"We're grounded in the car," he answered. "It's the safest place you can be."

The sky darkened a half tone, and a wall of rain closed off the horizon. "Yipe!" Miranda's father swung the Volvo onto the shoulder, parallel parking with other stranded motorists. Rain hammered the roof. The hazard lights in front of them were liquid and wavery. Beyond that, they could see nothing. Miranda capped her lens and realized that her father had said Grandma was his only living relative. Which was worse? That he seemed to forget Miranda existed? Or that she didn't think to call him on it?

After about twenty minutes, the rain slacked off and the cars around them came back to life. "That's the good thing about a tropical rain," Richard said as they plunged back into the tree corridor. "It passes so quickly. Look, the sun is coming out. Maybe we'll see a rainbow!"

"Oh, look, Toto!" Ariel mocked. "Everything here is so different from Kansas!"

Richard looked at her with real anger. "Do you want to know what John Knowles said about sarcasm?"

"Uh-uh." Ariel rooted in her purse. "Want a Life Saver, Miranda? Since we don't get any food till Grandma's house."

"John Knowles said, 'Sarcasm is the protest of people who are weak.' "

Ariel jerked around, withdrawing the candy roll Miranda was reaching for. Yellow and green circles rolled across the console. "I am not weak! And don't you ever think you can talk to me that way, Doctor, because I am not one of your patients!"

A shaft of sunlight pierced the sky. Something made Miranda look to her left and see a pink-and-green ribbon arching through the clouds. She grabbed the Nikon, tilted and fired. Maybe she could do a series on rainbows! What a great idea for black and white. Unless they wouldn't show up at all. "Is Grandma a good cook?" she asked. She had only visited her grandmother once, when she was four or five, and didn't remember anything about it. After that, her mother died and then there had been some kind of big blowup that went on until this past spring, when Lila invited them to spend the summer. Miranda planned to investigate the whole quarrel by pumping her grandmother for information.

Richard was making a turn. "She's a fabulous cook. She loves to cook."

"I bet she's gonna hate me," Ariel sighed. "You guys! Look!"

Suddenly they were beside the Atlantic Ocean. Just like that. It was a jolt! Miranda had trouble catching her breath. She had only seen the ocean on TV, and this was nothing like the placid turquoise beach of *Baywatch*. This was such a deep blue it appeared black, churning and foaming, rising up and slapping itself, roaring so loudly the sound penetrated the sealed car. "Open up!" Miranda knocked on her window.

"And the roof!" Ariel cried.

The windows opened and a fresh, weedy-smelling wind tumbled in, ripping Ariel's chignon to shreds, rattling the road map. A seagull flew beside the car, bobbing like a marionette. Miranda fired a shot and came to the end of her roll. "Shoot!" She fumbled in her duffel bag.

"I think I'm going to cry!" Ariel said. She had grown up in Los Angeles.

There were more shots than Miranda could catch—palm trees, beach people, boats, surfers. She visualized the black-and-white results and was thrilled—the black waves, edged in silver white, the turbulent swirls of gray sky, the gulls like handkerchiefs, floating over dunes. "Daddy, you were right! The real Florida is beautiful!"

Richard was swerving out of his lane, craning his neck to look at the ocean. "Thank god!" he said. "If we'd been in those hammocks a minute longer, I knew you girls were going to mutiny on me! I can't even recognize landmarks anymore, everything is so built up. I hope I can see the road to the causeway. . . ."

Miranda realized she was the odd one here. Ariel and her father had both grown up with beaches. Only she was a true city person. "When you guys were kids, did you hang out on the beach?"

"I did," Ariel said. "We'd get out of school and go straight to Santa Monica until dinnertime. And the same thing on Saturdays."

"On Saturdays, I'd walk around the island," Richard said. "All the way around the perimeter. It took all day, but it was a different experience every time. All the little coves and inlets, the marina, the marsh where the birds had nesting grounds . . ."

"Wow," Miranda said, although she couldn't really picture it. What kind of birds? Normal birds like she knew or giant pink flamingoes?

"Here's the causeway." Richard's voice was low.

It was a long silver bridge. The car swung east into a

magenta sunset. The rails of the bridge flashed above tangerine water. Miranda almost regretted not having any color film.

A flock of something like pterodactyls slowly flapped across their path.

"What . . . ?" Miranda squeaked.

"Pelicans, sweetie," Ariel said. "We had those in California. But when we get to the real Florida birds, you'll have to ask your dad. I don't know an egret from a spoonbill."

"I'm afraid I've forgotten it all." Miranda heard a quaver in her father's voice. "See ahead?" he asked. "There's Turtle Island."

An irregular landmass resolved on the horizon. A striped lighthouse stood to the right of the bridge above a collection of white sails bobbing in the water. The rest of the island was a murky canopy of trees. The east was purple now. All the birds had left the sky.

Miranda capped her lens and stowed the Nikon in her duffel bag.

Ariel's manicured hand rested on Richard's shoulder. "Does it feel like home, Rich?"

He nodded, apparently unable to speak. His free hand came up to touch Ariel's. Miranda wondered for the millionth time what to make of her father's second marriage.

The bridge came to an end and they were on the island, winding down dark residential streets. Miranda realized there were no streetlights.

"Grandma's house is at the far end of the island," Richard said. "The marsh area. You won't be able to really appreciate it in the dark."

Ariel was caressing his shoulder. "Was Jasmine from the island, too?" Jasmine was Miranda's mother.

"No, I met Jazz in college in Gainesville. She came from Tampa. Different world."

"The trees look spooky," Miranda said.

"Spanish moss," her father said. "These are mostly cypress, some live oaks, a few sea grapes—god, it seems like another lifetime!"

"It was, Rich." Ariel's fingers squeezed gently and let go. She turned to Miranda in the backseat and winked. "I guess we're not in Kansas anymore, are we, Toto?"

"Yeah."

The island was almost free of traffic, magnifying the croaks and squeaks in the woods. A half-moon edged between the clouds and silvered the moss-fringed trees. Something in the woods called out like an oboe.

They turned onto a new road, deep in the woods. At the end of that road stood a large white house with a pillared veranda, with some kind of shack off to the side. A pickup truck sat in the gravel driveway. Behind the house was a wall of cypress with a big spreading tree of some kind in the center. *Good composition,* Miranda thought, *horizontal and vertical.*

"This is it," Richard said. "Home."

Ariel flicked open the vanity mirror and began feverishly repairing her hair. "How do I look, you guys?"

"Great," Miranda said. "I promise."

Ariel turned around. A perfect white tooth bit into her perfect red lip. "Not like a bimbo or anything?"

"Don't be silly," Richard said. "Mom's going to love you."

It was contagious. Miranda ran a hand over her own spiky haircut. "Do I look all right?"

"Of course," her father said without turning around. "Listen, you guys. Mom is eighty years old. She's had a heart attack. She won't be that much aware of things." He pulled onto the gravel and cut the engine.

The door of the house flew open and a plump woman in a printed sarong bounded out. "Richie!"

It must be a neighbor who's taking care of Grandma, Miranda thought as the woman trotted down the steps. A string of multicolored beads bounced in and out of her cleavage. *Grandma is frail and lying in a darkened room like I pictured her.*

But Miranda's father was struggling up out of the car and accepting a bone-crushing hug with the eager stiffness he always showed in times of emotion. "Mom," he said softly. "You look fabulous."

"Hug me back, you idiot!" the woman commanded. "The war is over!"

Richard broke down and cried. "Oh, Mom."

Miranda and Ariel got out of the car, shooting nervous glances at each other. Miranda stepped closer to her grandmother, firing off pictures in her head of the deeply lined, tanned face, the thick, wavy white hair pulled back in a loose knot. This woman looked about fifty and could not possibly have had a heart attack. Up close, she smelled like some kind of spicy flower. Miranda found herself drifting forward, almost wanting to push her father out of the way.

Her grandmother looked at her. "Oh, Rich! Is this Miranda?"

Richard moved aside as Miranda threw herself into the warm, scented flesh. "Grandma!" she said in a childlike voice.

The little woman hugged her and held her out for inspection. "She's beautiful, Richard. Just like Jasmine, only more boyish, you know? Those same gazelle eyes! Shame on you for keeping her from me all these years!"

"You're the one—" he began.

"Never mind!" A plump hand flew up. "I promised myself not to get into all that. Oh, my goodness, Richard, is that your new wife standing there looking terrified? For heaven's sake introduce me!"

Miranda had never seen Ariel look so scared, including at the wedding last year. Ariel tugged at her short-shorts and pushed impatiently at a wisp of hair. "Hello, Mrs. Gates," she recited.

"Call me Lila!"

Ariel mumbled something about being pleased, while she was squashed.

"You didn't tell me Ariel was a knockout!" Lila scolded her son.

"Mom!" He sounded irritated. "We sent you the wedding pictures."

Lila had now deserted them to peer at something in the flower beds. She seemed to need to be in constant motion. "You can't tell from wedding pictures," she said. "They filter them."

"Ow!" Ariel slapped at her neck.

"Mosquitoes!" said Lila. "We'd better go in. Once they get the taste of you . . ."

"I see that!" Ariel slapped her ankle.

Miranda loved the inside of her grandmother's house. Oriental rugs covered hardwood floors. The furniture was something warm-toned, like cherry or mahogany. A chandelier crowded with prisms hung in the foyer. Lila seemed to like crystal. There were bowls and vases everywhere, mirroring the lamplight and casting points

14

of flame on the walls. A wonderful smell, bread and garlic and vegetables, came from the kitchen. Miranda felt puzzled, trying to remember if their condo in Cincinnati had a smell.

"Sit down, sit down, dinner's almost ready, how about a glass of wine?" Lila disappeared through a beaded curtain.

"Wow!" Ariel stared after her.

"What does that mean?" asked Richard.

"It's a compliment." Ariel had perched on a footstool, but now she rose a few inches and rubbed the seat of her shorts. "Oh, jeez, I think one of those little man-eaters bit me on the—"

"Ariel, stop it!" Richard hissed.

"What are you so tense for?" Ariel asked.

"I'm not, but—"

"Here we are!" Lila rattled back through the curtain carrying a silver tray with a wine decanter and four glasses. The wine was a red that would have photographed black.

"No, Mom," Richard said as Lila poured a glass and gave it to Miranda. "She's only fifteen."

"So?" Lila said.

He adjusted his glasses. "We have an agreement she won't drink until she's twenty-one."

Lila handed a glass to Ariel. "Oh, for Pete's sake, Richard. Don't suck the life out of her before she finishes high school. Miranda, when you're in my house, you may have the occasional glass of wine."

Miranda could smell it. It was a fascinating smell. She looked at her father.

"Go ahead," he said, scowling.

Miranda sipped. The flavor was strange, almost medicinal instead of fruity as she'd expected. Warmth burned the back of her throat. "It's good."

Lila handed Richard his wine. "If she becomes an alcoholic I'll take full responsibility. To your health." She poured her own glass and saluted them all.

"Speaking of which," Richard said. "Are you sure you had a heart attack, Mom? You look so healthy."

Miranda took a deeper drink. This one tasted different, like cherries and the musty smell of old books. She noticed how soft and beautiful the lamplight was.

"I've been taking walks and eating right," Lila said. "I'm going to get as much mileage out of this body as I can. But I'll come right out with it, Richard. The doctor says there was a lot of damage, and sometimes I can feel it. I'm at a point where I wouldn't buy any magazine subscriptions."

"Mom!"

"Oh, don't act horrified. I'm eighty. I've lived. I'd be perfectly happy to die right now. I don't like the way people treat dying like some dirty little secret."

"You're not going to die, Mom," Richard said.

16

"Have it your way, dear. I'm immortal."

Miranda had worked her way almost to the bottom of the glass. The taste was wonderful now, like blackberries and boy-kisses. Without actually moving, the room seemed to be slipping around a little. She wished she'd gone a little slower. She glanced at Ariel and noticed she was trying to discreetly squirm in her seat, scratching her mosquito bite.

Miranda laughed loudly.

Everyone looked at her.

"I'll go get our stuff out of the car." Miranda set her glass down. "I think I need some fresh air." She hurried to the door as the room looped and swung around her.

The night air seemed to help. She stood on the porch steps, making sure nothing was spinning, staring into the deep Florida night. The moon was melon colored, casting a glow on the clouds behind it. A breeze played in the treetops, swinging the moss like silk shawls. Miranda thought she smelled the same spicy scent her grandmother wore. Somewhere, far off, a dog howled.

She walked slowly to the car. Maybe this summer wouldn't be so bad after all. She opened the left rear door and took out the essentials—her camera bag and Ariel's makeup kit. As she leaned over, there was a soft snap behind her. A twig under someone's foot?

Twisting around, she bumped her head. She stood still, breathing hard, scanning the shadows. Her eyes were drawn to that shack. It had seemed like a toolshed at first, but it was more like a little house, with a door and two windows. But there were no lights on inside. The noise had come from behind the house, the marsh.

She noticed that her heart was beating fast. "Is someone there?"

Crickets chirped. The dog howled again.

It's the wine, you moron. You're drunk and weird. Go back in the house and try to act normal.

She hurried up the steps, feeling a familiar tension in her legs. She always felt that way when she knew someone was watching her.

two

Miranda opened her eyes. She'd been dreaming about a swing set—she was a little girl on a rusty swing, *creak-squeak! creak-squeak!*

But now she was awake on the sofa in her grandmother's spare room and the swing set was still creaking and squeaking.

Sitting up, she shook her head to clear the dream away. Her eyes were drawn to the window. Some kind of huge, fat blackbird sat on the outside sill, staring in at her. He did a weird maneuver over and over, puffing himself up and letting his feathers settle back into place. The morning light edged his black feathers with blue.

"Are you doing the mating dance for me?" Miranda

asked, wondering just how strange Florida wildlife was going to get.

As if he heard her, the bird immediately changed programs. Now he let out with a piercing *jeeb! jeeb! jeeb!* and then made a noise with his beak like castanets. His little eyes were as clear as pebbles.

Miranda jumped up, tugging down the shirt she slept in. "Shoo! Scat! Get out, you Peeping Tom!" She strode to the window, waving both arms. The bird bounced on his powerful-looking legs and flapped across the yard, landing near a group of his friends who were strutting around the big central tree.

In fact, the backyard was full of birds. The central tree, which was directly across from her window, had been turned into some kind of bird multiplex. Miranda counted six silver tubular feeders hanging from the branches, as well as two little wood "house" feeders. There was another thing that looked like a red plastic flower and seemed to be filled with liquid. Other parts of the tree held platforms with apples and corncobs in different stages of nibbling, and there was one thing that looked like a wire cage full of peanut butter.

While Miranda watched, a flock of something like pigeons or doves descended, settling in the branches and gracefully taking turns at one of the feeders. Their feet were an amazing shade of pink. Did they know that one feeder was theirs? She found herself hypnotized by their maneuvers. She rested her hands on the sill and let her body relax. It felt so good, it made her wonder how tense she was most of the time.

She scanned the rest of the yard. A redwood picnic table and benches. Glass wind chimes painted with pink flowers. Beyond the tree was the marsh—acres and acres of reeds and tall grasses with ribbons of water sparkling through. The sky was a deep turquoise, with one little spray of white cloud.

Miranda felt a tightness in her chest, the way she sometimes felt when she was trying not to cry. *What's your problem? Your dad grew up here. Not you.* But that was how it felt. As if she was remembering something.

Suddenly she needed to go out there and be in it. She rooted in her duffel bag for a pair of shorts, fingered her hair into place and automatically picked up her camera, then put it back again. *I'm on vacation. I don't have to record everything like it's going to disappear.*

Miranda stumbled over something in the hall. Her foot came down on something soft and squishy. *Mrrrr-OOOOOOOWWWWW!* It was her grandmother's gray cat, which had apparently been sleeping outside the door. *Like a guard,* she thought. What was its name? Weasel? "I'm sorry, Weasel," she said to the crouching, glaring animal. "I'm not used to a house with cats strewn all over it."

Weasel stared at Miranda long and hard, then opened his mouth and let out a slow, defiant hiss.

"Have it your way," Miranda said.

She noticed that her grandmother's bedroom door was open but the guest room, where her father and Ariel were sleeping, was still shut. Not surprising. Miranda was used to their fondness for "sleeping late" on weekends. Now that they were on vacation, they'd probably miss breakfast every day.

Looking carefully for additional cats or booby traps, Miranda picked her way down the shadowy hall and into the living room, which was a burst of light with its white walls and uncovered windows. The cut glass and prisms made little rainbows and sparklers on the walls.

"Miranda, is that you?" her grandmother called from the kitchen.

"Yes . . ." She hesitated to say "Grandma" to an almost-stranger.

"I was just going to take some coffee out to the yard. Grab a cup and join me."

Miranda smiled. "You read my mind."

"And the grackles prefer the sunflower seeds—that longish tube is for them. The sugar water, in the flower tube, is for hummingbirds, although I've never seen one of them. But butterflies and wasps come to drink it."

Lila paused to catch her breath and sip her coffee. The breeze billowed her caftan, which was streaked in yellow and orange, like marmalade.

"You're feeding wasps?" Miranda giggled. "It's a wasp feeder?"

Lila spread her arms. "I'm offering food. Anyone who appreciates it is welcome. Now tell me what you've learned so far."

Miranda pointed to the shiny, squeaky blackbirds. "Boat-tailed grackles." She swiveled her finger. "Mourning doves. White-winged doves. Turtledoves. Blue jay, obviously. Red-winged blackbird." She pointed out toward the marsh. "Ibis. Coot. Least bittern." Finally she shaded her eyes and pointed overhead, where a large bird was circling. "Osprey."

"Excellent!" Lila slapped the picnic table. "You take to it just like your father."

"I can't imagine him ever being into wildlife and stuff." Miranda sipped her coffee. Normally she didn't like coffee, but with Lila it was different.

"Oh, there was a time . . ." Lila seemed to go off into her thoughts for a minute. The wind chimes tinkled. Lila glanced at them, as if they'd waked her up. Then she looked at Miranda, studying her. "You should go explore the marsh. There's a lot to discover out there."

"Yeah. I'd like to set up some shots in my mind.

There's so much here I want to photograph. Including you."

"Me!" Lila touched her heart. "No! Take pictures of something pretty. Wait till you see the marsh at sunset. The colors are unbelievable."

"I don't use color," Miranda said. She always liked the shocked reaction this brought.

"What?"

"No, I believe in the purity of black and white. It forces the viewer to focus on the concreteness of objects."

Lila laughed. "Sounds heavy! Seriously, do you really want a world where everything is concrete?"

Miranda blinked. "You make it sound like I can choose what kind of world to live in."

Lila blinked back. "Don't you think you can?"

Miranda couldn't find an answer. Just then, one of the boat-tailed grackles alighted on the edge of the picnic table.

"Oh!" Miranda squealed softly. She had never been this close to anything wild in her life. The grackle cocked his head this way and that, as if looking at her from several angles. She realized after a minute that he was looking at her first with one eye, then with the other.

"He's so beautiful," Miranda whispered. The grackle

took a step toward her—gazing. He planted his feet and leaned toward her, stretching his neck forward.

"Is he telling you anything?" Lila asked.

Miranda thought somehow that this was the same bird that had been at her window this morning. She stared into the pebble eyes, trying to hear a message, and then she realized how crazy she was being. And how crazy her grandmother apparently was!

The bird suddenly pulled his head back. He glanced at Lila and then flew off.

"You'll do better the next time," Lila said.

"Do better at what?" Miranda wondered if her grandmother was teasing her.

"Let's change the subject." Lila set her cup down gently. She turned her gaze to the marsh, eyes narrowed against the climbing sun. The lines in her face were deep, like those of a smoker or sunbather. "Tell me about Ariel and your father."

Miranda's shoulders stiffened. "What about them?"

Lila turned back. Her face was so warm and friendly, it made Miranda want to tell her things. "You know what I'm asking. Is it a good marriage? Did Richard make a mistake? Is Ariel a good person?"

Miranda shrugged. "Who am I to say that?"

"You're an honest, smart, observant person whose opinion interests me. But you don't have to answer if

you don't want to." Lila's blue eyes were frank and friendly. Miranda thought her grandmother genuinely liked her but on the other hand didn't seem to care if the feeling was returned.

"Ariel's an okay person. I mean, I didn't really know my mother, so I don't have all that usual baggage . . ."

"What do you mean you didn't know your mother? Of course you did. You were five when she died."

Miranda wanted to change the subject. "About Ariel . . . she's the kind of person . . . people look at her and judge her . . . like a jealousy or . . ."

"I know." Lila nodded.

"And they don't pay attention to who she really is. And she's been reacting to that all her life, I guess, so she's worked out this . . . sort of tough-girl routine. To protect herself."

"Right," Lila said. "I worked out this . . . sort of flamboyant routine. Your father has a thoughtful-and-deliberate routine. Everyone has a routine."

Miranda didn't think she had one. "But anyway, none of that is the real Ariel."

"So what is?" Lila's eyes were narrowed with interest. Miranda was reminded of the grackle straining forward.

"Well, she worries a lot about what people think . . . how she comes across. She's always asking me what fork to use or whether this or that eyeshadow is tacky. It's because Dad's a doctor and we have money, she thinks we know all the inside secrets on how to live. She's right in a way. If we go to a party and there are other doctors' wives, they watch her, like they're trying to catch her out. I think because she's so pretty."

"I know all about this," Lila said. "My father was a shrimp fisherman, and then I married your grandfather, whose ancestors basically founded this island. And there was all this land and money, and my mother-in-law would look at a piece of jewelry I was wearing and I'd almost hear a buzzer go off. Wrong! You lose! It was horrible. Finally, of course, I realized that wealthy people are just as insecure and ridiculous as everyone else, and then I did whatever I wanted. I take great pride in doing what I want."

"You should talk to Ariel," Miranda said.

Lila smiled. "I fully intend to."

"What was my mother like?" Miranda asked suddenly.

Lila's whole face changed, and Miranda felt conspicuous. She hadn't realized how vulnerable she had made herself look. "Oh, honey," Lila said.

"It's no big deal," Miranda said. "You can't miss what you never had. That's what Daddy always told me. My memories are real vague. And people hardly talk to Daddy about her because he gets upset. I've seen pictures of her, and she's pretty, but she's a stranger. But I'd like to know what you thought of her."

27

Lila stretched as if the very memory of Jasmine relaxed her. "I knew her very well. I loved Jasmine. She was a wonderful person." She reached across the table and took Miranda's hand. "In many ways you remind me of her."

Miranda felt a sweeping urge to cry. She reminded herself that this was a woman who expected her to talk to blackbirds. Slowly she pulled her hand away. "I'm going to take that walk now."

Lila smiled. "All right."

Miranda looked at the shimmering mass of water and reeds. "There's nothing dangerous out there, is there?"

Lila continued to smile. "Everybody's idea of danger is different." She got up and went into the house.

Miranda hugged herself. Something in the yard had changed the minute her grandmother had left. She realized the birds had all flown away.

A dry leaf cracked under Miranda's foot, startling her. Her spine was rigid. This was an alien environment—she didn't know what to expect.

She had followed a grassy trail that threaded through the wetlands. Water stood on both sides of the path, choked with an abundance of plants—tall, dry grasses; spongy, ropy leaves the birds could walk on. Lily pads with cuplike blossoms rose on thick bouncy stalks. Flame-colored dragonflies hovered in the already hot morning air. There was a dry, herbal smell, mixed with the scent of water.

The sounds were what bothered her; unpredictable flurries of honking, trilling and cackling from the bird colonies. The incessant hiss of wind in the dry grasses. The sudden splashes of water, which Miranda would look at too late and see only the rings spreading.

Birds were commonplace, although Miranda felt a little pang of delight at each new sighting. The water was full of coots, which were like small ducks with eyes that didn't show up in their dark faces. They coasted beside the bank, pedaling their webbed feet, honking like little taxis. The flock of ibis she had seen from her grandmother's yard crossed her path several times, searching the grass for insects. Lila said they were storks, but they weren't tall like the cartoon storks Miranda knew, which flew around with babies in their beaks. She saw another grackle, sitting on a bush of red berries, fanning his long blue-black tail.

A few more steps and a huge white bird rose from the grasses and flapped across her path. She froze, holding her fist to her chest. She had never seen any bird so big, so close. She had heard the beating of its wings! She tried to memorize details to tell her grandmother later.

29

The bird was snow white and flew with his neck doubled, his head resting back on his wings. He looked like a piece of origami.

The sun was blazing hot. Miranda was tempted to pull her T-shirt off, but she hadn't bothered with a bra this morning, and even when she was alone, she felt shy. It was something Ariel had noticed when they shopped together. Ariel would choose a short halter dress without batting an eye. But Miranda would cringe in the dressing room if her shorts were too short or her V-neck too deep. It was just the way she was.

She ruffled her spiky hair with her hand. The back of her neck was sweating. As she tilted her head down, she saw a ripple near her feet. Snake! Her whole body reacted, springing back and stiffening, muscles locked. Electric shocks danced in her blood. The snake was all black; long, narrow and fast! It slithered diagonally across the path and slid up into a bush, winding itself in the branches.

"Oh!" Miranda gasped, trying to exhale her tension and disgust. "Jeez!" She rubbed her arms hard with her hands, as if the snake had showered her with cooties. Maybe it was time to go back. She took a few more halting steps, trying to ignore her pounding heart and ragged breathing. What if that thing was poisonous? What if there were more? Or worse things, like alligators? Surely her grandmother wouldn't send her . . .

A huge shadow covered Miranda, and something big dropped from the trees, landing with a thud in front of her.

Already jarred, she screamed, her arms flailing. It was bigger than she was. It was a man! A boy. Her age or maybe older. He was big, muscular, dark, foreign-looking, sweaty. All he wore was a pair of ragged cut-offs. His hair hung straight to his shoulders. Miranda could hardly breathe. *Run! Run!*

"You're kind of jumpy, aren't you?" he said.

Miranda took a step back. He smiled. She wondered how far the house was, but she didn't want to turn her back on him. Would a scream carry back to the house? Or would it make him go crazy, grab her, cover her mouth? *Quit thinking and just run, you idiot! Run!*

He shifted his weight, cocking his head. "If you want to wander around here, you need to get used to snakes and things jumping out at you." He laughed softly. His eyes were so dark she couldn't see the pupils. A rivulet of sweat trickled down his chest.

Suddenly her rigid body came unstuck. She pivoted and began racing toward her grandmother's house.

"Wait!" yelled the boy. "Hey, wait!"

Her tennis shoes battered the ground. She used her whole body to run, pumping her fists, sucking air into her lungs. Her side ached. Startled birds scattered on

31

both sides of the path. "Grandma!" she screamed as she ran. "Daddy!

He was running after her! She heard his feet pounding the ground, a pace faster than hers. Panic spurred her.

"Hey!" he hollered. "Hey!"

He was closing the distance, but the marsh was ending and the house was growing bigger. Miranda saw a jumpy image of her grandmother, coming out the back door, looking startled.

"Help!" Miranda shrieked.

"You bitch!" the boy panted. The voice was close.

Richard and Ariel, looking disheveled and sleepy, seemed to spill out of the house as Miranda thundered into the yard. "Call 911," she gasped. "He's trespassing. He . . ." She stumbled into her father's arms, choking, gasping. Her father passed her into Ariel's arms.

Through a screen of her tears and Ariel's blond hair, Miranda saw her father take several steps into the yard, like Gary Cooper. The boy came to a dead stop.

"Don't you move," her father said in a low voice. "Don't you even think about moving a muscle."

"I . . ." The boy was out of breath.

"Mom, go in the house and call 911," Miranda's father said.

The boy backed up.

"Freeze!" Richard screamed.

The boy froze. He looked at Lila with scared eyes.

"Richard, I'm sorry, but I can't call 911," Lila said. Her voice sounded calm, almost amused. Miranda twisted in Ariel's arms to look at her grandmother.

She was laughing. Lila was laughing. *God,* thought Miranda, *she is crazy.*

Miranda's father half turned, his face red with rage and panic. "Why can't you?" he screamed.

Lila giggled. "Because he lives here."

CHAPTER

three

They stood like chess pieces, making shadows in the grass.

"I guess you didn't tell them about me," the boy said to Lila. His hair lifted when the breeze blew, like the moss in the cypress trees.

Miranda pulled out of Ariel's protective embrace, trying to decide whether to stay angry or be embarrassed.

"I thought I'd tell them today," Lila said. "I didn't know you were planning to scare Miranda to death before breakfast."

He lowered his eyes. "She scares pretty easy," he murmured.

Just you wait, Miranda thought. The sun made sharp planes of shadow on his face. He looked Spanish, maybe, or Asian. He was muscular and tanned, like someone who spent all his time outside.

Miranda's father, who had been staring at his mother, suddenly exploded into motion. His arms waved. "Who the hell is he?"

Lila coughed delicately, as if her son had done something slightly embarrassing. "Everyone," she said. "This is Adam. Adam Fitzgerald."

Fitzgerald? Miranda had never seen any Fitzgeralds who looked like that!

"Well, we're all very pleased to meet him." Miranda's father was using the superrational voice that signaled he was on the verge of hysteria. "But would you mind telling us why he's living here with you? Mother?"

"He lives in the gardening shed," Lila said, pointing to it. "He's the gardener. And he does all the heavy work for me, runs my errands, drives me into town. What did you think, Richard? After a heart attack I'd be out pulling weeds the same as always?"

While this exchange was taking place, Adam "Fitzgerald" had raised his eyes to Miranda's. She thought she'd never seen such an unreadable expression in her life. He could have been furious or hot for her or on the verge of tears. It was something intense like that. She looked away.

Miranda's father paced up and down in front of his mother. "No, Mom, it all makes sense. I'm just slightly curious why you never mentioned him on the phone or why you didn't bring him up last night!"

Miranda realized Ariel had been awfully quiet. She turned, and there was no one there.

Lila was now using a sarcastic voice equal to Richard's. "Well, come to think of it, why was I keeping this dark secret from you? All right! He's my lover, Richard. Oh, I know it's mad, insane, but we just can't help ourselves. In fact, if you must know, that's why my heart is so bad. From making wild, passionate love to Adam in the gardening shed!"

Adam guffawed.

Miranda glared at him.

Miranda's father closed his eyes. He took several deep breaths. "Well, I think at the very least Adam should apologize to Miranda."

"What for?" Lila said. "He didn't mean any harm."

Miranda's father put his hands on his hips. He and his mother faced each other with exactly the same stance, squared off like dogs. "Because it's the polite thing to do and I'm sure Adam is a polite boy." He turned to Adam. "Aren't you?"

Adam offered his blank look to Miranda's father, then looked to Lila for instructions.

"Oh, go ahead," Lila said. "So we can get on with the day."

Adam stared at Miranda's father one second longer

than he needed to, then turned to Miranda. "I'm sorry, Miranda," he said. "I didn't know you were afraid of boys."

Miranda's father started to speak, but she held up her hand to stop him. "I'm not afraid of boys," she said quietly. "As long as they act civilized and don't jump out of trees like savages."

His gaze never wavered, but his chest rose and fell sharply. Twice. He turned to Lila. "You want me to take the truck over to Rob's now?"

Lila was blushing for some reason. A terrible, unbearable thought surfaced in Miranda's mind. About Adam's dark eyes and long hair and severe face.

"Yes," Lila said softly. "Tell him to check the air filter while he's at it."

"Okay. You want anything else from the mainland?"

"No. That's it."

He turned and strode toward the truck, head down.

"Oh, god," Miranda said to Lila. "Is he an Indian?"

"His mother was a full-blooded Cherokee. But you didn't know when you called him . . . that word."

The truck engine revved up.

Miranda sprinted toward it without thinking. "Wait!" She grabbed the passenger-door handle and yanked it open, propping one foot inside.

"Move," he said. He was staring straight ahead, squinting as if the sun hurt his eyes.

Miranda swung herself up into the passenger seat and closed the door. Faintly, she heard her father shout something. "Let's go," she said. "Before he gets involved. I want to talk to you." This should show him she wasn't afraid of boys!

He looked at her. His eyebrows almost met in the middle. "Get out of here!" he said. "Are you trying to get me in more trouble?"

"I want to apologize," Miranda said. "Let me go wherever you're going and we can talk."

She felt the door beside her open. Her father stood with his arms folded. His glasses had slid down his nose. "Miranda? What in the world do you think you're doing?"

Miranda swiveled to face him. "I was rude to Adam and I want to apologize. I thought I'd ride along with him to the garage or whatever it is."

"Jesus Christ," Adam muttered.

Miranda's father made a little noise between a bark and a laugh. "Can't you just quickly apologize and get out of the truck?"

"Yeah," said Adam.

"I was rude to him. I want time to explain."

Miranda's father exhaled at her, then leaned sideways to look at Adam, who was hunched over the steering wheel. "Adam, I'm sorry we all got off on the wrong foot. I'm sure you're a very nice young man. But you can understand that since I just met you, I don't want my daughter to just think she can jump in—"

"How are the peace talks coming?" Lila asked. She elbowed her son aside and held a credit card out to Adam. "I don't know how you thought you were going to pay Rob."

Adam accepted it, blushing. "He'd run a tab for me."

"I don't do business that way. Since Miranda's going with you and it may be a while, why don't you take her over to the Wharf for lunch? My treat."

"What is this?" Adam said. "She jumped in this truck by herself. I'm trying to get her out! Now you want me to take her to lunch?"

"Mother!" Richard said. "I don't want her roaming all over—"

"I don't roam!" Adam shouted. "And I don't want her here anyway."

Miranda took her turn. Somehow her grandmother seemed to be the judge of this debate. "I said something really stupid to Adam. I want to apologize and be sure he understands."

"I accept your apology!" Adam said. "Now you can go!"

"Adam, for heaven's sake!" said Lila. "Now you're being rude again. If this keeps up the two of you will spend the whole day apologizing to each other! Be polite. Maybe she'd like a little tour of the mainland."

"I'm going to Rob's garage in the middle of a slum!" Adam said.

"That's why I suggested the restaurant," said Lila patiently. "But have it your way. While you're in town, I want you to stop at Rexall and get me a lipstick. Maybelline Extra Long Wearing Frosted Cherry. Can you remember that?"

Adam laughed. "Lila, you just now made that up! You know I'm not going to go into a store and buy some lipstick."

"If anyone would like to hear my opinion . . . ," said Miranda's father.

"If you don't want to buy it, Miranda can get it. You see? You need her. Look, the two of you are going to become friends this summer. Why not get started now? I thought young people liked to spend time together away from their elders."

"Oh, I give up!" Miranda's father stalked off toward the house. "Do what you want!" he called over his shoulder.

"Is he talking to me?" Lila said. "Well, anyway, you kids run along and have fun." She shut the passenger door.

"Yeah, right." Adam put the truck in gear. He carefully maneuvered past Miranda's father's Volvo and swung out onto the little two-lane road. "You always pushy like this?" he asked, keeping his eyes on the rear-view mirror. His expression seemed to be a mixture of humor and anger.

"No," she said, pulling her knees up and hugging them. "Hardly ever, in fact. I don't know what got into me."

"I think you take after Lila," he said. He leaned back in his seat and propped one arm out the window.

"How did you get to know her?" Miranda asked.

He grinned, still keeping his eyes on the road. "I thought you wanted to apologize to me, not ask questions."

She smiled. "If I apologize, will you answer my questions?"

Finally he looked over. His eyes were playful now, almost sparkly. "If it's a good enough apology."

Miranda found herself noticing his legs in these close quarters. Smooth, muscular, not a lot of hair. She and her girlfriend Ginger had a ratings system for male body parts, and this guy would get a 10 for legs and at least a 9 for chest and shoulders. He was sitting on the rest of his score, but if that came out all right, he'd be a candidate for the coveted Golden Babe Award. In two years of mall cruising, Ginger and Miranda had only bestowed the award (unbeknownst to the recipients) two times. Miranda began to realize that her motives for coming along on this jaunt weren't totally pure. "Well, I'm sorry," she began. "I didn't realize at first that you were an Indian . . . I mean a Native American."

He turned down another road. They were taking a different route than the one her father had used last night. Or else everything looked different in the daylight. The canopy of trees met over the top of the road, grazing the hood of the car with lacy shadows and flashes of sunlight. The houses were small and weather-beaten, set far back from the road.

Adam gave a mock frown. "So it's okay to call me a savage if I'm a white guy, but not if I'm an Indian? I mean, Native American."

"Well . . . yeah."

He laughed. "It's no problem. I've been called a lot worse things than that anyway. I was really kind of mad because of the way you ran away from me. I was just fooling around. I didn't know I was so big and ugly girls would run away from me like that."

Miranda couldn't tell if he was genuinely insecure or fishing for a compliment. "You startled me," she said. She put her arm out the window. A wonderful free feeling spread in her chest. She was on vacation! In Florida! Riding with a good-looking guy! "You have to understand I'm from Cincinnati. This marsh stuff, all these grackles and snakes . . . it's like another planet to me. I was just getting over the snake episode . . ."

"She was just a little coach snake. She didn't mean you any harm."

"She didn't tell me that! And then you drop out of the tree like . . . Tarzan . . ." Miranda wondered if she had said too much. She'd thought of Tarzan because of the loincloth, and Adam's cutoffs were just about as brief. He didn't change expression, though. Guys never had a clue what was in girls' minds.

"Well, I'm sorry." He chuckled. "Next time I jump out of a tree at you, I'll wear my tuxedo."

"Okay." Miranda sat back and enjoyed the wind rushing through her hair. They were approaching the bridge to the mainland. In the daytime, the marina sparkled; sunlight on the water, bright white sails, the lighthouse like a big candy cane.

Adam pointed. "Right there is where we're going for lunch. I used to work there."

"Waiter?"

"Busboy."

"Oh."

"It's okay. The restaurant business wasn't my life. I was just trying to survive. I'm where I belong now."

He seemed nice and relaxed and open now, ready for interrogation. "Lila said you were Cherokee."

"On my mother's side. My father was Irish."

"I thought down here it was Seminoles and things."

"Seminoles, Tegesta. I'm from Tullahoma, Tennessee."

"Oh, we're practically neighbors. What's Tullahoma like?"

"Like where they'd send you if you're too bad for Hell," he said with a perfectly straight face.

"So you came to Florida to get away from Tennessee."

"I came to Florida to get away from my father. But getting away from Tennessee was a big bonus thrown in."

The sound of the wheels changed as they drove onto the long silver bridge. Bright water flashed all around them.

"Did you, like, run away from home?"

He looked at her, then away. "I walked away," he said. "Nobody was exactly chasing after me, begging me to stay. My mom died when I was a little kid."

"So did mine."

He glanced over again. "And my dad and I didn't get along. All we had in common was drinking, and that gets old."

Miranda was surprised at how much he was telling. He'd seemed like a private person. Maybe she'd passed some kind of test with him. She sensed, though, that it was time to get off painful subjects. "So how'd you meet Lila?"

"She wanted to sell this pickup and I wanted to buy it. See, I'm very good with plants, and I thought if I had a truck, maybe somebody would hire me as a landscaper, and, you know, a trade like that builds on word of mouth." He looked over for a nod. "And I thought if I did some good work I would build up a business, and I wouldn't have to be looking at people's dirty dishes and living . . . well, if you want, we're going to my old neighborhood. I can show you where I was living, if you think you can take it."

"Of course I can take it! What do you think I am, some kind of pampered little—"

"It's just rough, that's all. Some people don't like to look at things that aren't pretty."

"Well, if you could live there, I could certainly look at it."

"Okay, your wish is my command." They had crossed the bridge, and he swung the car down a narrow street, almost an alley. There was a boatyard, then a junkyard, then a county-run blood donation center. A line of people was waiting for it to open. Children played in the street, and Adam swerved around them without honking.

"This isn't so bad," Miranda said.

"This isn't it yet."

They drove past a building that looked burned out. Paper and masking tape covered the windows. Someone had spray-painted RICK over the door. Miranda looked ahead now, to see what was coming up next. The street they were on was winding. "So you went to buy Lila's truck and you ended up working for her?"

"I must have seemed like such a little jerk. Seventeen years old. I looked like something the cat dragged in. Talking big about starting my own business. Lila has this way about her—I can't explain it, but you'll see. You want to tell her things. I said I could only pay ten dollars a week at first, but I'd speed it up as soon as I started getting jobs. My job at the Wharf was at night, so I could have worked all day if I wanted to."

"And killed yourself."

"It'd be worth it. But she said wait a minute. I was just the kind of person she was looking for to take care of her property. We fixed up the shed so it was pretty nice—I'll show it to you. The whole situation was perfect. Lila believes in destiny and all that. Sometimes I do, too. Hey, watch where you're going!" An old man, who had been hanging on to a stop sign, lost his grip and slid into the street. A paper bag fell from his hand, and a bottle rolled out. "I hate that," Adam muttered. "Worse than anything."

They were now in an area of shacks, all built the

same in a way that looked suspiciously government regulated. The houses sat on sand, with no grass or landscaping. Children played with naked dolls and feral-looking dogs. But the residents had done everything possible to personalize their houses. Every front door had some kind of mural or slogan painted on: JESUS IS MY HELP, I HAVE A DREAM, KEEP OUT, ATTACK DOG. Some had flowers, peace signs and birds painted over the door. "Poor people are very creative," Adam observed. He braked suddenly in front of one of the shacks. It was smaller than the toolshed he lived in now. "Home Sweet Home," he said. The house was painted bright blue and said PIECES over the door.

Miranda tried not to let her voice gush with sympathy. "What's *pieces* mean?"

"The guy before me," he said. "He was a Pisces. He couldn't spell it."

Somehow this detail put Miranda over the edge. "It must have been horrible for you, living here."

He started the truck up again. "No, it wasn't at all. It was my house and I could afford it all by myself and I could keep it clean and not worry about drunken relatives coming in the middle of the night and ruining my sleep. It was wonderful."

"Well." Miranda tried to choke down her tears, since they were a kind of insult. "You should be proud of what you've done."

"Lila's done a lot of it. You need one person to believe in you or you never get out of these kinds of places." His voice was low and thoughtful. "All these people who live here, who knows what they can do? But if nobody ever takes a chance and helps them . . . oh, shit, I guess I should run for governor. Anyway, while I lived here I made friends with Rob, who runs the garage down the street here, and he's the best mechanic in the world, so that was good for Lila. She hadn't been taking care of this truck at all."

They pulled into the garage, which had Rob's name posted on every available space. It was really Rob's house, with the driveway widened for car work, but there were about twenty cars there in various stages of deconstruction. A blond guy in a Harley tank top crouched beside a Toyota. A German shepherd sat next to him. The blond man looked up at the sound of Adam's truck and waved. "Hey, chief!" he called. The dog barked. "Be right with you!"

"No hurry!" Adam called back. He turned to Miranda. "He's got a Coke machine. You want one?"

"No. I want to ask you something. You and Lila are friends, right?"

"Definitely."

"Do you know what the fight was about between her and my father? It was ten years ago. Does she ever mention it?"

Adam looked at her. "Yeah, I know about it."

"I need to know," Miranda said.

He reached for the door handle. "Then ask your father. Ask Lila. It's not my place to tell you. Okay?" He didn't wait for an answer. He jumped down from the driver's side and started around, maybe to help her out.

She made a point of jumping out quickly by herself. "It's important to me," she said.

"I'm sorry." He walked past her, toward Rob. "Why don't you go inside?" He gestured to the house. "There's a place to sit while we're waiting." He walked away from her. Angry as she was, Miranda took note of his final score—another perfect 10.

"That your girlfriend?" Rob called to Adam, grinning at Miranda.

"I'm working on it," Adam said. He held out his hands to the German shepherd.

Miranda was angry, even though she knew he couldn't have done otherwise. She walked across the gravel drive and let herself in the screen door of the house. Instead of a living room, Rob had a "waiting room" with plastic bus-station couches and a TV bolted to the floor. An inch of black fluid sizzled in the bottom of an ancient Mr. Coffee. There were no magazines. Probably Rob's customers weren't big readers. Miranda looked at the TV screen, where some channel was showing *Psycho*.

Adam came in after a few minutes with two cans of Coke. "I got you a pop anyway," he said.

Miranda accepted it, popped the top, and held the can to her forehead. Another thing Rob didn't have was air-conditioning.

"He said it should only be about twenty minutes. He thinks we're on a date, so he's giving us priority."

"Good. Adam, I know you won't tell me, but just tell me one thing."

"Oh, jeez!"

"Please. Did my father do something bad?"

He looked at her long and hard. On the TV, Anthony Perkins said, "We all go a little mad sometimes."

"All I can give you is my opinion," Adam said.

"In your opinion, did my father do something bad?"

Adam took a long sip of Coke and then turned to the TV screen, away from Miranda. "You better believe he did," he said.

CHAPTER

four

When the truck was fixed, Adam drove them to an ancient-looking Rexall. It was cool and shadowy inside and smelled like linoleum.

"You pick out the lipstick," Adam said. "I'm not dealing with any of that Crushed Cherries on the Highway business."

"Extra Long Wearing Frosted Cherry," Miranda said. She noticed that the girl at the cash register was eyeing Adam's shoeless, shirtless condition. Her flinty eyes had the unmistakable glint of a Rule Queen. She wore a lavender T-shirt with a big teddy bear on it.

Adam stared at the Revlon display. "There's ten thousand different colors! How do you keep it straight?"

"I don't use lipstick," Miranda corrected. She scanned the wall. "If I ever did, it would be something like this." She took out a tube of Natural Frost and displayed it for him.

"Looks like dirt," he said.

Annoyed, Miranda replaced it and took out another. "This is a color my stepmother would like. It's called Gladiola."

"I'd call it Hemorrhage. Hurry up, okay? I feel funny standing here."

"Who said you have to stand here? Go look at the jockstraps if you're feeling insecure."

He laughed. He also stayed where he was. "It's scary, the stuff women do."

Miranda hated conversations about the things "women" did. Most of the time they were things she wouldn't dream of doing. "Not just women," she pointed out. "Didn't the Native American men used to paint their faces for war?"

He laughed. "You got me there! Actually, they painted their faces for all different reasons. I was just reading this one thing about how they would paint their faces for certain ceremonies because they thought the red paint was attractive to spirits, like it would call them down. I'm trying to think how the book phrased it, it was cool. They said the paint would bring them to a window where they were visible to the spirits."

Miranda shivered. "That is cool." She realized she was staring at his eyes, which looked very beautiful when he was talking passionately. "Show me where the camera film is," she said quietly.

They had to go up to the cash register for that. The clerk was glaring at Adam now. "Do you want us to turn the air down for you a little?" she asked.

He looked at her with his nonexpression. "I'm fine, thank you, Lindsay. How are you?"

Lindsay exhaled, something just short of a snort. Miranda was distracted. "Hey! Where's the black-and-white film?"

"The what?" Lindsay was still glaring at Adam's chest.

Miranda grabbed the sales counter with both hands. "I need black-and-white film! I don't see any!"

Lindsay laughed, tossing back hair that was really too thin to toss. "Nobody uses black-and-white film around here, honey. Not since they invented color."

Miranda felt the walls closing in. Ariel was right. They were too far from civilization. She felt like a diver with a cut air hose. "Are you sure?" she said. "There must be some real photographers on this island some-where!"

"There's Ralph Stegner. But he uses color film. Who would want black-and-white wedding pictures?"

"I can't believe this!" Miranda knew she had lost it,

53

but couldn't seem to get it back. "I guess I'm lucky you even have four hundred film in this godforsaken . . . I guess I should be glad everybody here doesn't use Polaroids!"

"Are you buying the film or not?" Lindsay demanded.

"What's your rush?" Adam said. "I don't see a big stampede of customers waiting to buy things." He turned to Miranda. "I'll drive you over to the mainland tomorrow. And if we can't find what you want there, we'll keep going if we have to drive all the way to Miami!"

Miranda felt like a child, caught hopelessly in a tantrum, unable to back down. "I wanted to go out early tomorrow and shoot birds! I just can't believe this!"

"Buy her a candy bar or something, Adam," said Lindsay. "She's hurting my ears."

"Nobody's talking to you!" Adam told her. "Miranda, calm down. Can't you shoot one roll in color? I think they can convert color pictures to black-and-white prints."

Miranda felt her face turn red. It was like a hot, red spotlight on her cheeks. *She* was supposed to be the one who knew about photography. "That's right," she said. "Of course you can. I guess I can use this." She put several rolls on the counter along with the lipstick.

"Well, hallelujah!" said Lindsay. "Will there be anything else?" She turned to Adam. "A T-shirt? A pair of sandals?"

He gave her a charming smile. "What kinds of rat poison you got?"

White sails sliced into overlapping fields of aquamarine. It was noon and Miranda had to squint to look at the sparkling ocean, but she couldn't look away, either. She felt as if all her senses had been jarred awake by this new landscape—the blinding brightness, the heat on her face as they sat at the dockside table, the creak of ropes as boats rocked in the water and bumped gently together, the cries of seabirds. The complicated smell of the beach—salt, fish, coconut oil, and something subtle, like chestnuts or cigarette smoke.

Adam, whom all the waiters knew, had ordered grouper sandwiches, which sounded horrible to Miranda, but she was determined to choke it down and not act like a tourist.

Adam was lost in thought now, staring out to sea with his profile to Miranda. He wasn't one of those guys who made nervous conversation when things were quiet. He seemed to like the quiet. Miranda was free to stare at his bare arm, resting on the table; strong-looking but not too muscular.

Miranda pretended they were on a date. She pretended they had been going together forever and the Wharf was their place. They had had horrible fights there, had touched each other under the table when no one was looking. . . . They had been together so long they didn't need to talk anymore, everything was completely comfortable. Actually, that was the way it felt. Miranda placed her hand on the table, as close to his arm as she dared.

Adam came out of his trance when the sandwiches arrived. They turned out to be wonderful—flaky and white, not the whiskery sea monster Miranda had pictured.

"So you're a serious photographer, I guess?" Adam asked, squeezing lemon over his fish.

Miranda copied him, feeling like Ariel at a doctors' wives party. "Yes. I'm going to be a photojournalist. I've won some prizes already. I shoot only in black and white."

He had picked his sandwich up in both hands, but he put it down without tasting it. "Why?"

"Because I want to show the world the way it really is."

He sipped his Coke. "But it isn't. The world isn't black and white."

"Yes, but . . ." Miranda paused to take a bite of sandwich while she considered her answer. She had to think when she talked to him because he obviously listened. "What I'm trying to show in my work is the grimness of reality. I want to hit people in the face with the truth."

"Ouch!" Adam joked. "What do you say to people like me who don't think reality is grim?"

"I'd say grow up!" Miranda regretted that, but he didn't look offended. Still, she wanted to make up, so she said, "What about you?"

"When will I grow up?" he asked. "Probably never."

"No. What do you want to do with your life?"

A gull-like bird had landed on a post near Adam and was looking hopefully at his sandwich. "Wait your turn," he said to it. "You can have some when I'm done."

The bird flew off.

"If I gave him a piece now, he'd call all his friends and we'd be under a tern cloud in ten seconds," Adam explained.

"I was asking you about your ambitions," Miranda said patiently.

"Ambitions . . ." He took a bite and chewed it slowly. "Do you want me to tell you the truth? I'd like to keep on doing what I'm doing forever. Take care of Lila's property, feed the birds, see the eggs hatch . . ." He looked at Miranda, and apparently something in her face made him trail off.

She realized she was frowning. "You want to be a gardener the rest of your life?"

He leaned back, away from her. "In my way of thinking, there isn't any job higher than being a gardener."

Miranda felt scolded. They sat in silence. This time it wasn't comfortable.

"I know something we have in common," Adam said abruptly.

Miranda picked up her sandwich. "What?"

"We both lost our mothers."

Miranda looked off toward the water. "Oh, yeah."

"Mine died when I was born. How old were you?"

She looked at him. She didn't like this conversation, but it was his way of making up, so she didn't want to push him off, either. "I was five. So I didn't know mine, either."

He sipped thoughtfully. "Yeah, but you had a relationship with her."

"No. Not that I remember." Miranda felt uneasy, as if she were lying.

"Who doesn't remember things from when they're five?" he asked.

Miranda took a deep breath. She had said this speech many times, to teachers and other kids, anyone who wanted to help her talk about it. "Everyone's different, Adam. It's really a blessing that I don't remember very much. You can't miss what you don't remember."

"I think it's weird," Adam said. "Do you remember other stuff? Like, who was your kindergarten teacher?"

Ms. Miller. Long red hair wound up in a knot on top of her head. Loved to take her shoes off and walk around the classroom in her stocking feet. Told the class once she had wanted to be a ballerina but her bones were too heavy. Introduced Miranda to the Eloise books. Showed them how to make kites one day with construction-paper tails. "Not all that much," Miranda said. "Why are you questioning me like I'm on trial?"

"I'm not, I'm not, I . . . what did she die of?"

"Cancer, I think Dad said. It's hard for him to talk about it."

"Doesn't your dad think it's funny you can't remember her? He's a shrink, I would think . . ."

Miranda was getting a headache, maybe from that bright sun. "No, he always said it was a blessing. It is. Why would I want to remember something sad?"

He shrugged. "Because it's a part of you. I'd give anything to have had my mom for five years. You could soak up all kinds of memories in that time. And learn things . . . What about pictures? You've seen pictures of her?"

"Of course I have. Some people say she looks like me, but she doesn't. She's really pretty, kind of wild-looking. Her hair always seems to be a mess. She doesn't seem like the kind of person my father would pick."

"What color were her eyes?"

"Adam, I don't know. What difference would that make?"

"I'm trying to help you remember."

"I don't want to remember!" she shouted, so loudly that the other people eating on the dock turned around. Several pelicans that had been approaching Miranda for a handout sidestepped quickly away, glancing at each other.

"I'm sorry," Adam said. "You . . ."

"I don't want to talk about it anymore. Okay?"

"Okay! I'm sorry. Really."

He pushed his plate aside. Immediately the bird returned to the railing.

"You remembered what I said!" Adam broke off pieces of fish and began tossing them in the air. Within seconds he was surrounded by a wheeling, spiraling flock, weaving in and out among themselves, catching bread and fish in their beaks. It was so beautiful, Miranda had to look away.

After lunch they walked on the beach. It was low tide, according to Adam. The sun was hot, and the surf rhythm lulled Miranda into a dreamlike state. Tiny, glittering shells paved the shoreline. As they walked she collected some, rinsing them in the surf and tucking them into the pockets of her shorts. "Don't you want any?" she asked Adam.

"No, I've got plenty at home," he said, laughing. He plunked himself down in the sand.

Miranda swept a place smooth with her hand and knelt cautiously. "You come to the beach a lot?"

"I like the marsh better." He shielded his eyes and looked up at the sun. "More diversity. Fewer people." He began to dig in the sand with his hands, scooping out a round hole. Water began to seep in from the bottom.

"You don't like people?"

He sculpted his tidepool, shaping it with loving strokes. His hair swished back and forth. "A few. I like birds better."

Miranda laughed but realized he was serious. She began to dig with him, slowly losing her worry about getting dirty as her clothes and legs and arms caked with sand. They could always wash off in the ocean, couldn't they? Miranda wondered if Adam had a girlfriend. "So you're eighteen?" she asked.

He didn't look up from his work. He was starting a channel at one end of the pool now, which was apparently going to be a conduit to the ocean. "Uh-huh. And you're only fifteen, right?"

She didn't like the word *only*. "How did you know that?"

Was he blushing? No, it was the sun in his face. "I think Lila said something about it."

And you memorized it. Miranda had to move because Adam was now a foot away, continuing his trench. Her eye was caught by a tiny, brown-and-white bird, running along the shoreline. It was actually scurrying, fast as a mouse. "What's that!" She giggled.

He looked up. "Sandpiper. They like to feed at low tide."

"So that's the thing you and Lila have in common, right? Bird-watching?"

He scooped out a double handful of wet sand and plopped it down. "Well, we come at it from two different directions. Lila's one of these rich ladies who get bored and take up a cause. In her case, it was the Audubon Society. I mean it was a natural. She married this guy who had a big marsh on his property. She told me when she was a young mother, she'd wheel the stroller out on the trails and feed the birds, watch them with binoculars. And you know, when you're around wild things for any length of time, they become a part of you."

Miranda looked up. It was such a beautiful phrase, she wanted him to repeat it, but he was on a roll.

"So Lila quit playing bridge and joined up with a bunch of other ladies and they'd put on their big hats and go to Tallahassee and yell at the legislature. She's influenced some important bills that protected the wetlands. Ask her. She's sad now because a lot of her old political friends are dead. New people come to the island and they want to invest and build things. To them, the birds are in the way."

This was the longest speech Miranda had heard Adam make. He had stopped digging and was looking into her eyes.

"That's too bad," she said.

He opened his mouth to say something else, then seemed to change his mind. He moved closer to the water's edge and began the final phase of his canal. Miranda felt she had made some kind of mistake, not reacted right. She crawled after him on her hands and knees. They were now sitting in wet sand. When the waves rolled in, the foam lapped at their legs.

Adam finished his channel and sat back. "Now me," he said. "I have this half-assed approach of trying to be an Indian." He held his hands out to the surf, waiting for a wave to rinse them.

"You *are* an Indian!"

"Yeah, sure, but what do I know about the culture? I never knew my mom. I don't know any of her family because they were mad at her for marrying my dad. I was raised by an Irish guy. Where could I learn about Indians? From John Wayne movies?"

Miranda laughed.

"Or the museum? Where they have some arrowheads and a peace pipe mounted on the wall? Or school? I'd get these scraps, try to piece them together. First the Indians are good guys, helping the Pilgrims make popcorn; then suddenly we're the scourge of the West and we torture people and the Texas Rangers wipe us out. Other kids in school were scared of me sometimes. I could see it. Like you'd look at a wolf or something. I didn't know shit about what Indians believed, you know? Did they worship corn and dance around? I didn't know. So I started reading everything I could find. Black Elk—"

"Who?"

"He was a Lakota who fought in the Indian Wars. When he was old, he told his life story to a white guy and they published it, so for once it's Indians talking about Indians. That book was a breakthrough for me. Now I'm collecting books on the Cherokee people so I can know about who I am."

"So what have you learned? I mean, I know Indians worship nature and animals, right?"

"They honor nature. They see all creation as equal, not with man on top, but . . ." He locked his fingers together.

"Interdependent?"

"Yes! So that's where Lila and I come together. I think . . ." He stopped and looked at his hands, which had been describing arcs in the air. "Oh, god, I must sound so stupid! I don't go around making dumb speeches like that all the time. Why didn't you shut me up?" He was blushing now; it wasn't the sun.

"I was interested," Miranda said. "I see now what you meant about being a gardener."

He smiled. A large wave rolled in and surprised them both, splashing Miranda's face and soaking Adam's shorts. Water rushed up Adam's canal and flooded into the tidepool. They both watched. When Miranda turned back to Adam, she jumped, because his face was very close. His eyes were half closed and his mouth was partly open. She felt his hands clasp her shoulders. She closed her eyes. His mouth was warm, the pressure even and gentle. The darkness behind her eyelids was red. The sun burned into her back. Another wave struck them and receded, leaving them dripping.

Finally he let go. He looked out to sea. "I didn't want you to think I was all talk," he explained.

five

Adam nearly ran over Ariel. She was sunbathing in the driveway, stretched out on three pink bath towels in her black bikini. Her blond hair fanned out like a halo.

"Jeez!" Adam said, hitting the brakes so hard it almost tossed Miranda off her seat. "I could have killed you!" he shouted out the window.

Ariel rose on her elbows and propped her Wayfarers back on her head. She grinned, flashed Adam a peace sign and lay back down.

"Flake," Adam muttered, jerking the emergency brake.

Miranda jumped down from the passenger seat.

"Here!" She tossed the drugstore bag to Adam. He caught it, along with the hint that he was supposed to go into the house alone.

Ariel sat up again, smiling. "Your boy's high-strung."

"He's not my boy," Miranda said, sitting on a small edge of the towel. "But guess what? He kissed me!"

"You're kidding! I don't believe it!" Ariel put her hands to her face in mock amazement. "You're telling me an eighteen-year-old boy spent the day alone with a fifteen-year-old girl and they kissed? Unheard of!"

"Okay," Miranda said. "But it was possible he wouldn't like me, right? That does happen."

"Not to pretty girls like us." Ariel smoothed Miranda's bangs. Even though Miranda liked the gesture, she pulled back. "Is he nice?" Ariel asked. She gathered her hair in one hand and held it off her neck, letting the breeze blow through.

"He's hard to read," Miranda said. "But I like him. He's passionate about things."

"You already told that part of the story."

"No, I mean serious things like ecology." Miranda reduced her voice to a whisper. "He was really poor before he came here to work for Grandma."

Ariel laughed. "Hey, I wasn't exactly Ivana Trump before I met your dad, either."

"No, I mean bad poor. He lived in a shack on the mainland."

Ariel shrugged. "So? It's what's in here that counts." She tapped her heart.

"Right," said Miranda. "I agree. Why are you sunbathing on a gravel driveway?"

"Because I tried the grass and about five thousand tropical bugs swarmed over my body. So far, this vacation is the pits."

"There's a beach, you know. I was on it."

"Fine for you. Your dad got a call from some old jerk school buddy and off he goes with the car. Didn't even ask me to go along. And you take off with Sitting Bull for the whole day, so where did that leave me? Alone in the hive with the queen bee!"

"Lila's nice," Miranda said.

"I'm sure she is! But I don't know her and I'm the second wife! I don't relish spending my first day getting scrutinized. This woman starts rolling out dough before noon! And when she's not cooking and baking she's out in the swamp, counting alligator eggs or something. I'm in heavy culture shock."

"Poor baby." Miranda giggled. "We'll go on a shopping trip to Miami in a couple of days. Okay?"

"Forget Miami. I need Palm Beach to get over these blues. I'll never be this close to Worth Avenue again, and I'm not going to miss it. I can feel the stores calling to me now . . ." She held her hands out like a sleepwalker. "Chanel! Gucci! Cartier!"

"Jeez, you're hopeless. I'm going inside." Miranda stood up and brushed herself off.

"I figured you'd abandon me for that handsome young boy."

"Who wouldn't?"

Ariel laughed. "Call me when dinner's ready."

As she walked up to the house, Miranda glanced back at Ariel. The setting sun washed her long body in pink, making her gold hair seem even brighter. Miranda had never in her life known anyone so Hollywood beautiful. And she knew, with a pang of embarrassment, that this was one of the reasons her father had married Ariel. He loved her, but her armpiece value was clearly important to him. Why then had he left her here alone when he could have shown her to his old school buddy?

Inside the house, Miranda was dizzied by the cooking aromas. She headed straight for the kitchen, where Lila was stirring a pot on the stove. She wore a sarong printed with cherries. Miranda had never seen a woman this age show so much cleavage. Sensing something, Miranda looked higher and saw that cat—what was his name?—sitting on top of a high dish cupboard. As usual he glared at Miranda, his eyes as bright and cool as philodendron leaves.

"What are you cooking?" Miranda asked. "It's killer!"

"Oh, hi." Lila turned and smiled. "I have crab cakes

in the oven and this is wild rice and in the other pot I'm steaming some mustard greens. And I baked corn bread a while ago."

"I love you, Grandma," Miranda said, giggling.

Lila laughed. "Somehow that sounded more like 'I love food.' Did you have a good lunch?"

"Yes." Exploring, Miranda had found the corn bread, cooling on a blue plate under a dishtowel. She broke off a corner and popped it in her mouth. It was so rich, it tasted buttered. "We had . . . groper? . . . sandwiches."

"Grouper!" Lila laughed. "One of my favorites. The Wharf has its own fleet, so that was this morning's fish you were eating. Nothing like that."

Miranda pulled a stool up to the stove. "When we went in the drugstore, this very shabby girl . . . Lindsay? . . . was rude to us."

Lila examined the greens. "Lindsay Baker. She's not gifted with charm."

Miranda thought there was information here. Before she could lunge for it, Ariel appeared in the kitchen doorway, holding her towel in front of her, which seemed silly considering how Lila was dressed. "Do I have time to take a shower before dinner, Mrs. Gates?" she asked.

"Mrs. Gates?" Lila said. "The last person who called

me Mrs. Gates was a judge in De Land who sentenced me to three weeks' community service for civil disobedience." She turned to Miranda. "We were guarding sea turtle eggs and they said we obstructed the beach. The laws are different now." She swiveled back to Ariel. "Yes, go ahead. We can't eat until your runaway husband comes home anyway."

"Okay." Ariel backed away. In a second they heard the shower running.

"That kid is scared to death of me!" Lila commented. "Am I so frightening?"

"No," Miranda said. "But she's always afraid people are going to disapprove of her."

"Who could have an opinion?" Lila stirred the greens, banged the spoon on the side of the pan and propped it in an oyster shell she was using for a spoon rest. "She flits around here like a tall fairy. She hasn't lit anywhere long enough for me to get a good look at her."

"She'll calm down. So this Lindsay Baker . . ."

Lila laughed. "You're a sharp one, aren't you?"

"She's Adam's girlfriend?"

"Oh, no, nothing like that. They went out a couple of times last year, but Adam was never serious about her. What were you two doing that made her nervous?"

"Nothing. Just being there. Where's Adam?"

"He dropped off the lipstick and sprinted out the backdoor. I think he wants to put on a shirt for dinner, which I must say has never happened before. . . ."

"Oh!" Miranda said. "He's going to eat with us."

"Watch it. You're giving yourself away. I thought your father should get to know him better, so he won't be so jumpy about the whole thing."

"There isn't any thing," Miranda insisted.

"Of course there isn't. Would you take that lipstick back to my room and put it on the vanity table? Adam was in such a hurry to freshen up . . ."

"Sure." Miranda laughed and slid off the stool, snagging the bag on her way out.

In the hallway she collided painfully with Ariel, who was now wrapped in a bath towel. Ariel shrieked like a guilty felon. "Oh, it's you. I thought it was Lila. I forgot to bring my clothes to the bathroom. I'm not used to having it down the hall."

"Why are you so worried about Lila looking at your body?" Miranda said, rubbing a sore rib where Ariel's elbow had gone in. "Don't you see how she runs around?"

Ariel paused in the doorway of the guest room. "I don't want her to think I'm a slut." The door closed.

Miranda hummed Patsy Cline's "Crazy" as she dropped off the film in her room and then went down to Lila's bedroom. It was a neat, feminine room

72

with blue walls and a chenille spread on the bed. Set in the front of the house, a bay window overlooked the driveway and the road. There was a cute window seat with a bookshelf underneath. Miranda fit herself into the cozy space. Adam's little house was also visible off to the side. There was a light on inside, but Miranda couldn't see anything. Next she tried out the bench at Lila's huge vanity table, which also faced the window. At first she thought all the surfaces were dusty, but she concluded it was dusting powder, since that was clearly a favorite product of Lila's. There were several different boxes of it—all Avon varieties with elaborate designs. There was a black one, for instance, with gold filigree around it. Another was pale blue with two white doves on the lid. Another was shaped like a pink lotus blossom. A huge atomizer of Hawaiian White Ginger cologne sat front and center. Miranda sprayed her wrist and sniffed. Yes, that was Lila. The dressing table also held a number of small boxes: wood, glass, enamel. Miranda opened each one. Bobby pins, old-fashioned hair combs, scatter pins, ropes of colorful beads and large artificial pearls. Despite Lila's wealth, Miranda didn't see a single piece of "real" jewelry. And apparently the only item of makeup Lila liked was lipstick. She had a rack of them, every shade of red, pink, peach and mauve you could name. Miranda slotted in the new cherry tube.

She was just about to start trying on beads when she heard a car outside. It was her father. She instinctively ducked her head so that he couldn't see her through the window. He got out of the car looking worried. Or maybe the right word was *guilty*. Miranda wondered if his old school friend was male or female. He locked his car, tugged his clothes fiercely, shot a poisonous look at Adam's house, went back to check his car lock and started for the house again.

Miranda sprinted down the hall to greet him at the door. "Hi, Daddy!" She gave him a big, friendly hug and a kiss on the cheek.

"Hi." He looked distracted. "I'm glad to see you back here in one piece."

Miranda swallowed that and countered sweetly, "Where have you been?"

Lila came out to the dining room with a stack of plates. She distributed them loudly around the big oval dining table. "Well! There you are at last, Richard. "How's Skip?" The name Skip was pronounced like the recitation of a plague.

"The same," Richard said weakly, then switched to the offensive. "Five plates? I thought Adam ate in his own house."

"Sometimes Adam eats with me, and I thought it would be nice to invite him tonight," Lila said, smiling. "Since he and Miranda are hitting it off so well."

"What does that mean?" Richard cried, wheeling toward Miranda.

Miranda shrugged. "What it sounds like, Daddy. I like Adam. We had a nice day together. Who's Skip?"

"Do I look all right?" Ariel emerged from the shadows of the hall in a white sundress with spaghetti straps. Between her and Lila, Miranda was starting to feel flat-chested.

"Where'd you get that?" Richard asked.

"Lazarus. You've seen it before." Ariel looked wounded.

"Don't you have a little jacket or something to put over it?" Richard's jaw muscles were twitching.

"Listen here—" Ariel began.

"You never said who Skip is," Miranda said.

The doorbell rang.

Ariel started for the door.

"You don't need to answer the door, honey." Richard hooked her arm and held her back while he moved forward. "I'll do it."

Adam stood in a swarm of moths from the porch light, dressed in a worn white button-down shirt and jeans. His hair was pulled neatly back. "Hello, Mr. Gates," he said in the same tone Ariel used for Lila.

"Come on in," Richard sighed, backing up.

"Thanks." Adam looked at Miranda and blushed. "Hi, again."

"Hi, again," she said. She realized she was grinning in a goofy way and stopped it.

Lila came in with two platters of food. "We're ready! Hello, Adam."

"Hey, Lila." Adam and Richard started for the same chair, both backed off, then came forward again and looked at each other in exasperation. Miranda felt queasy.

Ariel chose a seat and smoothed her skirt carefully. Miranda sat to her left. Adam hurried to the seat next to her. Lila came in with the corn bread and took the seat next to Adam. Richard sat down between his wife and mother. Everyone watched steam rise from the food.

Ariel laughed nervously. "So this is what it's like to have a family," she said.

Lila smiled. "Yes. I came from a big family. It was just like this. We all watched each other around the table like fighting cats."

Adam laughed, but no one else did.

"Why don't you tell us about your day, Richard?" Lila asked.

Somehow this was a signal for everyone to move. Plates were picked up and passed.

"It was nice," Richard said, keeping his eyes down. "It's always nice to see old friends."

Adam's foot nudged Miranda's under the table.

Richard cleared his throat. "You know we went all

through high school together and he stood up with me when I got married, so it really isn't surprising . . ."

Adam withdrew his foot, suddenly all business. "Is this Skip Wilson we're talking about?" he asked Lila.

"Yes." Lila was staring a hole through her son.

Ariel and Miranda shrugged at each other.

"What does *he* know about Skip Wilson?" Richard demanded, hooking a thumb at Adam.

Lila's chin lifted. "He's my friend, Richard. He knows a lot of things."

Adam looked at his plate.

"Who is Skip Wilson?" Miranda exploded.

"He's a friend of mine from high school," Richard said.

"He's a lot more than that," Lila said.

Ariel raised her eyebrows at Miranda. Miranda shrugged again.

"Let's drop the subject," Richard said, stuffing food into his mouth. "These crab cakes are great, Mom. I really miss your cooking."

Ariel sighed. "I try, Rich, I really do."

"I didn't mean anything about your cooking and you know it!" he snapped.

"What did you and Skip talk about?" Lila said. "Did he ask you how I was doing?"

Richard put his fork down. "Of course not, Mom. That's ghoulish."

"Your agreement with him is what's ghoulish!" Lila shot back.

"Mom, I thought we agreed to put this thing behind us and move on."

Lila stabbed at her food. "I'm trying to do that, Richard, but if you are going to spend part of your time down here with that man, how do you expect me to feel? It's like having a goddam buzzard circling my house."

Ariel had lost her patience. "Do you guys want Miranda and me to leave so you can talk about whatever this is?"

Lila looked at her warmly. "There you go! That's more like it! I knew you had guts the minute I laid eyes on you! Yes, Richard. Why shouldn't your wife and daughter know about your legal and financial dealings?"

Richard was doing something with his hands that looked like the old church and steeple game. "Well, I guess they should know more than what you've obviously told to outsiders." He glanced at Adam.

"I'm not an outsider, Mr. Gates," Adam said in a voice so quiet, it was disturbing.

"Go on!" Lila said to Richard. "Tell them. Tell them what you did if you think there's nothing shameful about it."

"There isn't, and I will." Richard sat back in his

chair. He spoke directly and exclusively to Miranda. "I guess you know your grandma and I had some kind of big fight a few years ago. I made a decision that made her very angry."

"I don't get mad, Richard," Lila said. "I get even."

He ignored her. "Skip Wilson and I went to Palm High together. We were best friends. I was kind of a skinny, shy kid, and Skip was the athlete. He wouldn't let other guys pick on me, you know?"

Miranda nodded. She thought this was an awful lot of background, which must mean he was leading up to something big.

"And I did things for him, too. It was symbiotic. He had a bad home life—his father was literally a monster, and he needed . . . someone to talk to. I was a good listener. It might have been from this friendship that I honed some of my counseling skills."

Miranda nodded again. She glanced around the table. Everyone was looking at his or her plate.

"We were as close as friends can be. He was the closest person in the world to me until I met your mother. . . . " Richard's voice wavered. He cleared his throat and continued. "Skip went on to be a very successful businessman. A developer. He took his father's failed construction business and made something out of it. It was like his final victory over the old man, you know?"

Miranda wished she could take a bite of food, but her father was holding her with his eyes. "Yeah, but I don't see—"

"He's developed this whole island," Lila said. Her tone was flat and monotonous. "Those hotels and high-rises by the marina, all the new houses you see on Sea-grape Avenue, all of that, Wilson Development. All we lack, according to your father's friend, is a mall. He says the island can never grow without better shopping facilities."

Miranda thought that made sense after seeing the Rexall, but she didn't say so.

"He needs a large piece of land for a mall," Richard continued. "A piece as big as—"

"Mine," Lila said sharply. "And he isn't going to get it. We don't need a mall, and my land is already being used. It's a nesting ground."

"Oh, Mom, for Pete's sake, the birds can go anywhere."

"That's where you're wrong!" Lila stabbed the air with her fork. "Thanks to self-made men like your friend Skip, the birds are running out of places to go."

"You have to weigh the relative benefits—" Richard began.

"Maybe she has," Adam said, keeping his eyes down. "Maybe her values aren't the same as yours."

Richard turned to Adam, his blue eyes hot and shiny. "This has nothing—and I do mean nothing—to do with you!" He paused and took some "centering" breaths, a technique Miranda knew he taught his patients. "Anyway, remember, Miranda, when we visited here? You were about five."

"I really don't."

"Well, we did. Your mother and I brought you down for a visit, and Skip came over and made a very generous offer to your grandmother and was even willing to make it an estate bequest, so she could live her life out here—"

"What a sport!" Lila huffed.

"Mom! So anyway, as you can see, she refused. Well, this is the thing, Miranda, that caused this . . . horrible rift between your grandma and me. A rift that I hated and regretted." He turned to Lila, who looked away. "Anyway, what happened was, Skip asked me if I would sell him the land after I inherited it. I said I probably would. I think this community needs to come into the twentieth century, and I—"

Lila interrupted. "He signed a paper saying that the very minute I drop dead this Werewolf Wilson can swoop in and start bulldozing my marsh and everything I care about."

"Mom!"

"That's the truth, isn't it? That's the truth, Miranda. That's how your father honors my memory. By selling me out before I even hit the ground!"

Richard flinched. "Mother, when it's my property, I have a right—"

"You're right, Richard. Legally, you had a right and you exercised it. And I had a right to stop speaking to you for ten years because I honestly didn't feel like it. What kind of son cares so little for—"

"I understand what the marsh means to you," Richard said. "But it doesn't mean that to me. I happen to agree with Skip."

"And you also happen to know you'd make a killing on the sale of this property, too, right?" Adam was still staring at his plate, but his whole body was rigid with anger.

Richard turned to him, red-faced. "I'm warning you for the last time—" he shouted.

"Excuse me." Adam's chair shot backward, and he seemed to be out the front door in three bounds.

Miranda, along with everyone else, turned her eyes from the door to Richard.

"Well, I'm sorry!" he said to Lila. "It was your idea to have him sit in on a private, family—"

"He is family to me," Lila said.

"Well, I just met him, so I don't—"

"Excuse me, too." Miranda pushed her chair back gently.

"Hey," Richard said. "What do you think you're doing? We're still talking about—"

"I want to see if he's all right."

"Damn!" she heard her father shout as she closed the front door.

The night air was a relief. Miranda felt hot and choked. She wasn't sure how she felt about any of this. She didn't want her father to be wrong. Ecology to Miranda had just been a nerdy fad in school, a fad during which kids wore whale T-shirts and picked up trash on the weekends. She didn't want to think about any of it. She was sorry they'd told her. It was a grown-up thing. She didn't care. She knocked on Adam's door.

"Miranda?"

"Yeah."

"Go away. I'm okay."

"Can I come in?"

"I'd rather be alone."

"I don't believe you."

There was a long pause. The door opened. "You're so pushy," he complained. "All right, have it your way. Your father will think I'm molesting you out here, but I

83

guess he hates me anyway." Adam began to pace. Miranda got the feeling he'd been doing it before she came and that it was a thing he did often.

"My father doesn't hate you." Miranda tried to study Adam's austere decor in the lamplight. The furniture—a bed, a table, a chest of drawers, two chairs and a bookshelf—all looked handmade, out of some kind of heavy-grained, reddish wood. His floor lamp had an amber glass shade, which made the room glow like a firelit cave. He had no bedspread, just a plaid blanket with the sheets and white pillows showing underneath. Nothing on his dresser top but a wooden hairbrush and a wooden box. Nothing on the tabletop. No pictures on the wall but one, a pen-and-ink of a crow, which hung above the bed. The bookshelf was too far away to read titles in this light. A bright rag rug covered the wood floor. The mood of the room was tranquil, almost meditative, and seemed incongruous with its occupant, whose angry pacing seemed to give off bolts of jagged energy.

He ground his right fist into the palm of his left hand. "I don't like your father," he said. "I'm sorry. I was going to try so hard . . . but he yells just the way my father used to." He stopped suddenly and looked at Miranda. "Does he drink? Does he hit you?"

"No! Of course not! He's not abusive at all. He was upset. I've never seen him this upset. It's because of all this stuff he and Lila are going through."

84

"She's right and he's wrong," Adam said. "You see that, don't you?"

"I don't have any opinion yet," Miranda said. "I just heard all this for the first time tonight. But I don't think a mother should stop speaking to her son just because—"

"Just because he can't even wait till she's dead to destroy all she has and desecrate her spirit, so he can add to his mutual fund portfolio?" He was pacing even faster, making such sharp turns, it looked as if he might topple over.

"Adam, it's their fight. I just came out to see if you were okay."

Finally he was slowing down. "I'm okay. He just . . . having any older guy yell at me always freaks me. The next thing I look for is a fist in the eye."

"He's not like that."

Adam walked over and stood close to her. "I guess I'm partly mad because I wanted him to like me. Because of the way I feel about you."

The room seemed awfully quiet all of a sudden. And hot. Miranda thought she could feel heat coming off Adam's body. "How do you feel about me?" she asked.

His eyes were like melted chocolate, just before he ducked his head. "You know."

She took a breath. "I don't know. Tell me."

Moving in closer all the time, he whispered, "I'm so bad with words, Miranda."

She put her arms around his waist and pulled him the rest of the way. Their bodies fit comfortably. She tipped her head back. "Okay," she said. "Show me."

CHAPTER

Miranda half knelt on the footpath, peering at the marsh through her viewfinder. No composition. She rotated her body to the right, where a cluster of wild hyacinths floated, breaking up the vertical lines of the saw grass. She angled up to include a spill of clouds with dark gold rims. Close. A coot paddled right into the frame. Like a hunter pulling the trigger at the right moment, Miranda tapped the button, feeling the whir resonate in her chest. There was no satisfaction in the world like it—not even the soft, gentle way Adam had kissed and touched her last night. Even that wasn't quite as thrilling as catching a perfect moment in time, making its beauty apparent to everyone who would ever see it—even a thousand years later.

The three of them were spread out over the trail, like a broken string of beads. Adam was impatient with photography and had hurried ahead. Miranda could see his lean figure on the horizon; he stretched his arms out as he turned in the four directions. He'd explained the ritual to Miranda, and she thought it looked beautiful. His shadow, as he pivoted and stretched, flowed like black water on the ground. She waited until he came to a still moment—facing west—and took a picture. The morning light kindled gold fire up his back and made the white front of his T-shirt blaze. His upturned face was copper, his hair as black as his shadow. He looked like something from another world.

Lila had lagged behind Miranda, leaning on her African storyteller's stick, plucking at the flowers and grasses as if they were part of a garden, stopping at nests to count the eggs. All morning Lila had been singing "Over the Rainbow" in her thin, vibrating soprano. Miranda could still faintly hear the song carrying above the rattling grass and whistling birds. " 'Where troubles melt like lemon drops, away above the chimney tops . . .' "

Miranda joined in, " 'That's where you'll find me . . .' " She decided to stay where she was and let Lila catch up. She looked at the path ahead, but Adam had vanished. Miranda savored her memory of last night. Adam's warmly lit room, his eyes, his hands. Miranda had a little experience with boys, but none with a boy this much older than she was. When Adam kissed her she could close her eyes and feel a swirl of gravity that seemed to pull her down. He had run his hands up and down her back, wanting to go lower, she had thought. Between kisses they had looked into each other's eyes. He had put his hands on her hips, and Miranda had swayed forward, pressing into him and feeling "it," and he had quickly grabbed her shoulders and pushed her back. "Okay," he had laughed. "Time."

"It's okay," Miranda had answered. "I know where to draw the line."

He had shaken his head. "You're a kid."

Any other guy saying that would have infuriated her. But the way Adam had said it, the word *kid* meant something precious, fragile.

"Well," she had said. "I'm growing up fast."

His voice had been hoarse as he'd said, "Good."

The sun was climbing fast now, searing the morning air. Miranda thought it was about ten o'clock. Her father and Ariel had gone to the beach today. He had been all jolly at breakfast, trying to smooth over last night. Miranda knew he was feeling outnumbered.

Something furry brushed Miranda's calf. It was the gray cat. "Hello, Wesa. Is Lila close behind?" She stroked the cat's spine, watching it rise to meet her hand. "Do you want me to take your picture?" Miranda had finally gotten the cat's name straight. It wasn't Weasel, it was Wesa, the Cherokee word for *cat*. Adam only knew a handful of Cherokee words, but the few he knew were special to him. When he moved in, Lila had let him change the cat's name from Pom-Pom. "If you were my cat I'd name you Max," Miranda said, trying to fit the cat's slithery shape into the viewfinder. Wesa twisted like taffy, propping his forepaws on Miranda's leg, sniffing the lens. In the viewfinder, he was a dark blob with a little pink nose in the center. "You can't photograph a cat," Miranda sighed, trying to push him back. It was like trying to push spaghetti.

The soprano trill resumed, much closer now. " 'If happy little bluebirds fly beyond the rainbow, why, oh why, can't I?' "

Miranda swiveled and found Lila in the viewfinder. "Hi!"

Lila struck a Mae West pose. "Hi." When the picture had been snapped, she rested on her stick. "Well? Are you in love with my marsh yet?"

Miranda blushed. For a second she'd thought the question was going to be about Adam. "I was from the first minute."

Lila scanned the horizon with satisfaction. "Can you imagine sacrificing all this for a mall? A mall? I ask you!"

Miranda thought of the things she'd seen this morning. The anhingas repairing their stick nest, turtles sunning themselves with one foot stretched out, bitterns tiptoeing across water lilies. She could almost hear the roar of bulldozers, see everything twisting and breaking apart, clouds of dust towering in the sky. "Maybe deep down Daddy loves this place, too," she said. "I think he does. I don't think he'd really sell it."

Lila was still gazing at the horizon. "I don't think he will, either. In fact, I'm not really worried at all." She looked at Miranda, almost said something, closed her mouth, then said, "Your father is a good man, Miranda. I was very angry with him at one time, but I'm not anymore. He just exasperates me sometimes. He's like his father in some ways—closed off from his own feelings. Sometimes I thought that was why he went into psychiatry. So he could let the other person talk and keep his own problems to himself."

Miranda waited for more, but her grandmother was squatting now, holding her hand out to the cat. Suddenly a little blackbird with red and yellow wing bars swooped out of a bush and landed on the path between Miranda and Lila. Its object was a small plumlike fruit that had fallen from a tree.

"Oh!" Miranda automatically raised the camera. Through the viewfinder she saw Wesa, dropping into a crouch, flattening his ears against his head. His eyes were evil slits. "Oh, no!" Miranda cried. "Look out!"

She dropped her camera and clapped her hands. The bird flitted off.

Wesa glared at Miranda.

Miranda put her hand over her beating heart. "That was close."

Lila didn't look even slightly upset. "Miranda, dear, Wesa hunts birds in this marsh all the time."

"And you let him?"

"Of course! How would I stop him?"

"Put a bell on him. Keep him in the house."

"But he wants to be out here hunting birds!"

Miranda sat back on her heels. "I can't believe you! I thought you loved birds. I thought your whole life was about protecting them. How could you just let your cat—"

"Easy, easy," Lila laughed. "First of all, Wesa is an animal, too. He happens to be a carnivorous animal. He was designed and built to hunt things. If I kept him in the house, that same blackbird would probably have been stalked and killed by a gator or a bobcat or a little boy with a slingshot. That bird decided to land a few feet from a cat. It lost its right to survive and breed when it made that dumb decision. Wesa only gets birds that are too slow or old or stupid to get away. That's how nature keeps everything running smoothly."

"That sounds so cruel!" Miranda protested.

Lila shrugged. "I've spent my whole life observing

wild things. And let me tell you, it's not like *Snow White,* where all the animals dance in a circle and throw flowers at each other. It's kill, kill, kill, day and night. The cats kill the birds, the birds stalk and kill the grass-hoppers, the grasshoppers probably kill something or they wouldn't be here. It's a savage garden, as they say."

Miranda stared at the cat. She didn't know how she felt about this. "Let's go catch up with Adam," she said softly.

"Okay," said Lila. "Go slow, the humidity is bother-ing me a little today."

They walked in silence for a while. Birdcalls meshed and tangled in the thick, sun-heated air, punctuated by the croak of an alligator.

"To me," Lila said as if there had been no interrup-tion, "the real crime is human beings, who are so arro-gant they think they can interfere and impose human morals on a world they know nothing about."

An egret sailed overhead. Miranda followed it with the camera until it angled away from the sun, then snapped it. "All day long, I've been photographing kill-ers," she said.

The three of them had lunch at the picnic table in Lila's backyard. Tuna, cucumber chunks and chopped red peppers stuffed into pita pockets, a salad of green grapes and strawberries. Lila gave away half her lunch, offering snippets of tuna to Wesa and tossing green grapes out onto the lawn for the grackles to fight over.

Miranda was still wrestling with the law of the jungle. "What if Wesa killed one of those grackles?" she asked. "They're almost like your pets. Wouldn't that make you mad?"

"Wesa doesn't even try for those grackles because he knows they're too fast and too smart." Lila swigged from an Evian bottle and made a face. "Ugh. Health. When I was young I had a martini every single day with lunch and a couple more before dinner. And sometimes a brandy . . ."

"That's why you have a bad heart now," Adam said. He was eating grapes with his fingers in a way that fascinated Miranda.

"Au contraire," said Lila. "A lot of studies will tell you a moderate amount of alcohol is good for the heart. I just happen to have a doctor who—"

"Alcohol isn't good for anything!" Adam insisted.

"You're an evangelist, Adam," Lila said. "And that's not very attractive in a boy your age. Anyway, Miranda, the point I'm trying to make about predators is that they serve a purpose and weed out excessive or undesirable birds. You know how people say cats are cruel because they play with their prey? What they're doing is being sporting. They give a healthy, smart catch every chance to get away. These grackles over here are smarter than most of the people I know and not above working in teams, either. Wesa wouldn't stand a chance, and, as you can see, he knows it."

It was true; Wesa paid no attention to the birds on the lawn. On the other hand, he was being hand-fed tuna at the moment. "They do seem intelligent," Miranda said. "Like that grackle that sat on the table and looked at me yesterday."

"He made an approach to you," Lila said. "Animals choose people according to their affinities. You might be a bird person, just like me. You agree, Adam?"

"Sure," he said with his mouth full.

"Maybe we should teach Miranda a few insider secrets?" Lila teased.

Adam shrugged. "Let the birds decide."

Miranda felt a jolt of discomfort. How wacky were these two? Had she stumbled onto a New Age bird cult? She remembered there was a picture of a crow in Adam's room. "Let the birds decide?" she cried.

"A great idea." Lila stood up. "Wesa? Let's go in the house." She gathered the cat in her arms. "Confident as they are, I don't think these boys will sit at a table with a cat." She carried Wesa to the back door, murmuring to him.

Miranda thought of a book she had read once about witches and their familiar spirits. "What's she going to do?" she whispered to Adam.

"*You're* going to do it," he corrected.

Lila returned to the table. "Now," she said like a schoolteacher. "Here are some pointers on grackles. They can't see out of both eyes at once, so they're always looking at two worlds. They can see life and death, so they know whether a still animal is asleep or dead. I'm telling you some ways they're superior to us, so you'll have more respect for them. They see more colors and more distance than you could ever hope to. They're wise and extremely fair, but they have a very subtle, almost malicious sense of humor."

"Grandma, you're nuts!" Miranda said.

"Do you agree with everything I just said, Adam?" Lila asked.

"Of course." He grinned. "Everybody knows this stuff."

"You're both nuts," Miranda said.

"Well, I guess you have to experience these things for yourself," Lila said. "Okay, here are the basic rules. Never follow or trail or stand behind a grackle. Never let them see you swallow. Hold still when they approach you, and don't make a fist or close your hand. Look at them in quick glances, not a steady stare. Talk to them and let them answer. Anything else?" she asked Adam.

"That's enough to get her started," he said.

"Pick up a grape," Lila said. "Put it in the palm of your hand and brace your elbow on the table comfortably, so you won't tremble or change position. There." She arranged Miranda's hand the way she wanted it, a perfect green grape balanced on the palm. "Now, tell those grackles over there you want to know them better and to send an emissary over to meet you. And mention the grape, of course, but don't make it the main thing."

"You've got to be kidding," Miranda said.

Adam grinned. "She doesn't believe you, Lila. Here, let's give her a demonstration." He took the grape and balanced it on his own hand. Then he turned to the grackles and made a clicking sound. They all looked up at once. "Hello, boys!" he said. "Would one of you come over and show Miranda how sociable you can be?"

The largest of them, with no hesitation, skipped forward in the grass, then soared to the table and landed on the edge. He glanced at Miranda and stepped around the table, making short turns, cocking his head to look through each eye in turn. Miranda had to cover her mouth to keep from giggling. Up close, the bird did seem to radiate intelligence. His eyes were sharp and fierce. He looked at Miranda more frequently than the others.

"You're staring at him, and he doesn't like it," Adam said to Miranda.

Miranda glanced away, then back, then away, then back, but she felt like a fool.

The bird picked up a crust of pita bread from Adam's plate and shook it.

"No," Lila said, pulling the bread right out of the bird's beak with a gentle motion. "Adam has a grape."

The bird looked at Miranda again, then at Adam's hand. He craned his neck forward, cocking his head and watching Adam. Then he swallowed, opened his bill, plucked the grape and, tipping his head back, tossed the grape in the air so that it dropped down his throat.

"Thank you!" Adam said. "Way to go!"

The bird had already taken flight, rowing the air with his long, blue-black wings.

"Pretty cool!" Miranda said. "So you guys have these grackles tamed."

"No way," said Adam. "They let us hand-feed them, but they're not tame. Did you see him swallow before he ate?"

"Yes." Miranda was still watching the bird as he milled around the lawn with his buddies. They all looked different to her now, like little feathered men.

"Most birds swallow before they eat," Adam was saying. "That's why it's bad manners to let them see you swallow. They think it means you want to eat them."

"And they know a lot of predators who stare, too," Lila said. "Cats, for instance. So when you stare at the bird, he feels stalked. Since we can't speak with them, we have to try to communicate in body language the best we can."

"Did you learn all this from a book?" Miranda asked.

Adam looked impatient. "We learned it from the *birds.*"

"I want to do it," Miranda said. She balanced the grape on her palm. "Here, birdies! Come and get a grape."

Adam shook his head. "Show some respect. You sound like someone setting a trap!"

Miranda laughed. "Would one of you fine birds do me the honor of eating this grape?"

To her surprise, one of the grackles—she would swear it was the one that had hung around her yesterday—left the pack and walked toward the picnic table, cocking his head back and forth, studying her. "Honk!" he said finally.

"He's interested," Adam said. "But he's not sold. Coax him."

Miranda was sucked into the drama, trying to do everything right, glancing at the bird and then away, refusing to swallow. "Please? Would you please take a grape from me?"

The bird bent his knees like a broad jumper and flapped into the air, landing lightly on the table. He looked at Miranda, then walked in a small circle, glancing back over his shoulder at her. She could hear his feet clicking on the redwood.

"I think he's jerking you around," Adam observed.

"Please." Miranda stretched her hand out further.

The bird lowered his head like a charging bull and raised his wings in the air like a caped vampire.

"What's that!" Miranda whispered.

"He's just showing off," Lila said. "This is the sense of humor I told you about."

"He can see how much you want it," Adam added, chuckling.

The bird suddenly straightened up, shook himself so that all his feathers puffed out, then let them slowly settle back into place. Then he stepped decorously forward, swallowed, took the grape, tossed it and swallowed it. He shot Miranda a final, ironic glance and flew off to the other birds, making loud clucking noises.

"He's laughing at me," Miranda complained, but she realized she was smiling.

The bird took off suddenly, wheeling up toward the sun. Miranda almost felt as if her heart went with him, flew right up into the sky. She touched the edge of the table as if to ground herself. She realized she was laughing like a child.

The clatter of whistles and calls from the trees was deafening.

CHAPTER

seven

Miranda sat on the Earth Day 1994 beach towel beside her father, watching a tern waddle along the shoreline. She used to think these birds were seagulls, but now she knew that the gulls left Florida in the summer. In the three weeks they'd been on Turtle Island, both Adam and Lila had been cramming Miranda's brain with flora and fauna facts. She was trained now; if she saw a new bird or unusual plant on the beach or in the marsh, she would memorize the details and go back to Lila's magnificent library to look up its name. As Adam said, "When you know the name of something, you treat it differently."

The terns were favorites of Miranda's. They looked like CEOs with a bald spot and tufts of black "hair" on each side. They seemed to take themselves too seriously. This one, for instance, looked almost disapproving of Miranda's stare and hurried along as if embarrassed. Miranda glanced at her father to make a comment and saw he was staring out into the ocean, where Ariel was swimming.

Miranda followed his gaze. Ariel was standing in the surf, holding up her arms like a goddess. Waves crashed around her thighs. Several men in the water and on the beach were staring at her. Miranda didn't like Ariel's bathing suit. It wasn't a thong, but it was a very high-cut two-piece with a big daisy printed over each breast. Miranda knew she was a prude about some things, but you could go too far the other way, too. This outfit made it seem like women's bodies were some kind of joke.

One of the men in the water said something to Ariel, and she laughed, throwing back her wet hair.

"You could tell her you don't like that," Miranda said, surprised at the harshness of her own voice.

Richard was surprised, too. He jumped. "She's having fun," he said. "Sometimes I feel like all I do is spoil her fun." He pulled his knees up. He looked kind of nerdy and vulnerable today; trunks showing off his skinny legs, his beeper hooked to the waistband in case Dr. Clothfinder couldn't handle one of his patients back home. He picked up the book he was reading, *Paradoxi-*

cal Crisis Intervention, and held it in front of his face like a screen.

Miranda watched the men watching her stepmother. Ariel looked like a movie star, bronzed and long-legged. Diamonds dripped from the ends of her hair. Miranda was about to yell "Shark!" when there was a funny noise beside her. It was Richard's beeper vibrating.

"Damn," he said. "I knew this lull was too good to be true."

Miranda was also surprised at how good his patients had been. Usually when he tried to get any time to himself, they all went berserk to make sure he wouldn't abandon them.

"It's local!" Richard said, staring at the number.

Miranda knew immediately. The beach tilted up around her. The sun made her blind.

Richard's face was slowly changing. "I hope it's not about Mom," he said softly, and got up, almost running to the pay phones.

The coronary care unit's waiting area at Gates Hospital was like a hotel lobby with sky blue carpet, rose-colored walls and baskets of silk flowers. A wide-screen TV featured *Oprah,* a show about a whole family who had taken out contracts on each other, all with the same hit man. The hospital was the most sophisticated thing on

103

the island, largely, Miranda knew, owing to her grand-father's donations.

Adam, who had been there the longest, was slumped so far forward, his hair obscured his face. He was strok-ing a little stone. Miranda didn't know if it was a reli-gious thing or just a nervous thing, and she was afraid to ask. He was completely freaked out on guilt, blaming himself for Lila's collapse. He'd been weeding around the sage plants, and Lila had come to help him. Even though he'd tried to stop her, telling her the sun was too hot, Lila had laughed him off. Then, when she'd slumped over, he had just picked her up and put her in the truck and driven straight to the emergency room, not even thinking to call an ambulance. When the oth-ers arrived, he'd been babbling these facts incessantly, like a criminal making a confession. Now he had fallen silent.

Ariel, Miranda and Richard had been there over an hour and hadn't even seen the doctor. Richard and Ariel sat side by side on a little sofa, holding hands and look-ing like two frightened children. Richard was still wear-ing his trunks and a silly Hawaiian shirt. Ariel had put a windbreaker over her bathing suit. They both wore flip-flops. Ariel's hair had air-dried and looked flat and mousy.

Miranda, who knew enough to put clothes in the car when she went to the beach, had so far eaten two bags of potato chips, a bag of white cheddar popcorn and a "honey-bun" from the vending machines. She was on her third can of Coke. Her whole body felt greasy and bloated.

"In an ambulance, they could have given her CPR," Adam muttered to himself.

Richard leaned forward. "You did the best you could," he said, for maybe the fiftieth time. "You reacted quickly, you got her here. It doesn't do you any good to second-guess yourself now."

Adam lifted his head. "But I—"

"And frankly, you're starting to annoy everybody," Richard added.

Adam laughed, then smiled shyly at Richard. "Thanks."

"Just one of the clever tricks I learned during my expensive education," Richard said. "Your problem is that you believe if you feel guilty enough it will help Lila, but it won't, so you might as well give it a rest."

"I know." Adam nodded. "You're right."

"She's strong," Richard said.

"She is." Adam ducked his head, then looked at Richard with a different expression. "How are *you* doing?"

In a calm voice, Richard said, "I'm completely losing my mind, just like you."

They smiled at each other. Miranda felt a wave of joy, thinking maybe they could get along after all. Then she felt guilty for thinking about such things when Lila was fighting for her life.

Finally the doctor came out. He was short and heavy and had a fuzzy, dark beard. He reminded Miranda of a teddy bear. Miranda held her breath and wondered if everyone else was doing the same.

"Hello, I'm Dr. Suzuki." He shook everyone's hand. "We have Lila's heartbeat stablized," he said. "For now."

Miranda heard them all exhale together.

Dr. Suzuki frowned. "But I don't want you to get overly optimistic, either. It took us a long time to get this arrhythmia under control. This isn't like the last time, when she bounced back quickly and adjusted well to the medication. Quite frankly, Dr. Gates, we've been having a scary time of it back there the last few hours."

Adam, who had stood up for the doctor, sat back down. His body seemed to deflate.

Miranda realized she was picking her cuticles to the point of making them bleed. She put her hands in her jeans pockets.

Richard lifted his chin high. "So what are you saying, Doctor?"

Dr. Suzuki ran his hands over his face as if he was tired. "I'm saying she's stable now, but I don't feel easy with it. I feel like I've spent the last two hours balancing a piece of china on a flagpole, and now it's balanced, but

I want to keep looking at it. We tried a different medication on her, and that was what did the trick. But the next forty-eight hours will be critical, and she'll need constant monitoring. If the heartbeat is stable after that, maybe we can breathe easier, but right now it's still a wait-and-see kind of thing."

Miranda's father touched the doctor's sleeve. "I appreciate your telling it like it is. Can we see her?"

"You won't like my answer to that. I know how all of you feel, but Lila's in a fragile place, as I said. If she sees you guys, she's going to want to sit up and talk, and that could upset the balance we've got. I know it seems cruel but I'm forced to say no, in the patient's interest."

"I understand." Richard looked down.

"Come back tomorrow morning after I've looked at her, say around eleven, and if she's okay, we'll see what we can do. I just want her to get through this night with no surprises. Fair enough?"

"Fair enough." Richard sat down. His eyes were unfocused.

Adam looked up suddenly. "Could we—I—stay here at the hospital tonight?"

Dr. Suzuki looked at Adam. "Are you her grandson?"

"No. I'm her friend."

Dr. Suzuki studied Adam's face. "If it makes you feel better, you can sleep here in the waiting room. My advice, though, is to go home, change clothes, get some sleep, try to—"

"No, I need to stay close by. I really need to." He looked at Richard for help.

Richard smiled at him vaguely. "You do whatever you have to, son."

Hearing her father call Adam *son* flooded Miranda with so many emotions, she didn't even try to figure out what they all were.

"Maybe I should fix some food," Ariel said, without enthusiasm. It was dusk. They sat in Lila's living room, watching little fires die out in the prisms as the sunset faded. No one moved to turn on a lamp.

Richard didn't answer. He'd been standing at the bay window for an hour, looking at nothing, keeping his back to his wife and daughter. His shoulder blades, under that dumb shirt, looked small and vulnerable.

Ariel had changed into a black tube dress and was on the couch, feet tucked under. "Maybe a drink?" she suggested.

"There's a lot of stuff I should have said," Richard told the lavender sky. "A lot of stuff."

"So?" Miranda challenged. "Tell her in the morning!"

He didn't answer. The sky behind him evolved into a

deep, phosphorescent blue. A small, tattered cloud, stained a tangerine color, drifted into view. Miranda was always annoyed with beauty when she was upset. It felt like a mockery.

"I'm going to have a drink," Ariel said. "Any takers?"

No takers. What Miranda wanted more than anything was to go out to Adam's house and be surrounded by his harmonious things, but of course she couldn't do that.

The telephone rang. Ariel, on her way to the kitchen, screamed. Miranda and Richard swerved their heads toward the phone like prey-smelling predators. Then they all looked at each other. The phone rang a second time.

"I'll get it," Ariel said. She went into the kitchen. Miranda and her father locked eyes while they listened.

"Hello? Who? Oh, hi. No, I'm not Miranda, I'm Ariel. Oh, thanks, that's nice to hear. Look, we're kind of in the middle of a crisis right now . . . yes, it's Lila, she . . . Do you want to talk to Richard? Let me see if . . ." She put the phone down and came all the way over to Richard. "It's your friend Skip," she whispered. "Do you want me to tell him—"

Richard almost pushed her out of the way, racing to the kitchen. "Hello? Hi. No, she . . ." Emotion flooded his voice. "It's another heart attack. I am. I am.

Oh, man, you don't know, it's been so . . ." he sobbed audibly. "Hello? Yeah, I'm sorry, I'm a mess. I just . . . could you? God, that would be great. They wouldn't even let us *see* her—" He broke off and sobbed again. "Thanks, man. Thanks." He hung up and staggered into the room, wet-eyed. "He's coming over."

Miranda felt her body snap into a standing position, almost against her will. "He what?"

The room was dark and full of shadows. Ariel drifted to a lamp and lit it.

Richard's face was red and blotchy. "He asked if I wanted him to come over."

Miranda felt something that might be rage pushing her lungs in and out. "Daddy, he shouldn't be here with Grandma in the hospital. She wouldn't want him here. It's . . . it's . . . ghoulish!"

"What are you talking about!" Richard exploded. "Skip is my best friend. I'm upset! He wants to come over and—"

"It's not right!" Miranda said. "That man is waiting for Grandma to die so he can get what he wants from you, and he shouldn't be here—"

Richard's eyes blazed. "I guess we see which side you've been listening to!"

"It's just not right!" Miranda felt she was about to cry herself. She and her father never shouted at each other.

"And what does this say about what you think of

110

me?" Richard's face was like the face of an angry child facing a parent, not the other way around. "Is that what you think, Miranda? Do you think I say to myself, Goody goody, Mom is going to die tonight and Skip can be right here to do the paperwork?" His voice had risen to hysteria. His eyes were scary, the red capillaries making the blue seem more vivid.

"Rich," Ariel said.

"I know what they've been doing to you!" Tears flowed from his eyes. "They've been working on you from both sides. So you would think I'm a complete monster. What has it been? Three weeks? And you're ready to sell me out already?"

"Dad, what are you talking about?"

"Thinking I'm a bad guy when you've only known me all your life, when I'm that guy who raised you all by myself when your mother died and made you French toast every single Sunday morning of your life, but watch out! A few picnics with Lila and that . . . that . . ."

"Don't!" Miranda felt like slugging him. Hard.

"It's fine." He put up both hands. "You think whatever you want, Miranda. But maybe you can see why I need my friends around me when I'm hurting. It's because my family . . ." He choked, turned and walked out of the room.

Miranda was breathing so hard, it made her dizzy.

She looked at Ariel. "I had a right to say it! It's Lila's house and she's struggling to stay alive and that man shouldn't be here right now."

Ariel hugged herself. "This always happens when there's someone in the hospital. Everybody turns on everybody because they're afraid."

"There's an issue here!" Miranda said. She felt frustrated. All the things she hadn't said were bouncing around inside her. "This is about what's right and what's wrong!"

"But he's hurting," Ariel said. "This is his mom, and he—"

"Then he should respect her feelings and—"

The doorbell rang.

"Oh, Christ," Ariel said. "Now what? That can't be him already."

"Don't let him in," Miranda said.

"Rich?" Ariel called. There was no answer. The bell rang again.

"I'm not going to let that man in." Miranda folded her arms.

"Why did I ever marry into this stupid family?" Ariel said. She tugged angrily at her dress and went to the door.

"Hello?" It was a soft, deep voice with a trace of a Southern accent.

Miranda had the urge to bolt, then the urge to stay, then another urge to bolt.

"Are you Skip?" Ariel asked.

"Yes. Are you Ariel? My god. Richard's description didn't do you justice."

"Come on in, we're a little . . . well, it was a bad day."

"I know."

Miranda didn't look up at first. She wanted his first view to be of an angry, surly adolescent.

"Miranda!" he said in his rainmaker voice. "The last time I saw you, you were a tiny little girl, and look at you now."

Curiosity made her look up. She could see right away why people would sell their land, or their souls, to him. He was lean and tall, maybe six feet three or four, with curly black hair and warm syrupy blue eyes. He was trying to dress like a regular guy—jeans and a blue chambray shirt—but the accessories, alligator boots and a diamond ring you could slug someone with, gave him away. This guy was all about money. Were the boots supposed to be a bad joke?

"I don't remember you," she said.

He acted as if he didn't hear the ice in her voice. "You look just like Jasmine except for the hair. Jasmine had wild hair like a Gypsy."

113

Miranda clenched her jaw, suppressing an urge to cry. She was about to run out the door when her father came in. His glasses were off, and his face looked red and raw in a way Miranda had never seen. He must have been crying freely, like a child.

Skip Wilson spun around, sensing or hearing him. "Oh, Rich." He shook his head. "You're falling apart too soon, here. She's gonna be okay. You know Lila. She's a fighter." He held out his arms, and the two men hugged. Something about the way they hugged let Miranda know this was a deep, trusting friendship. As a photographer, she needed to analyze what it was. It was the way they leaned their weight on each other. When people hugged perfunctorily, they kept their weight on their own feet.

"I'm so glad you're here," Richard said. "I'm sorry I haven't called. Lila was—"

"You always were an emotional jerk, Richard," Skip said affectionately. "Look, why don't we all have a drink and talk about how Lila's gonna outlive all of us put together."

"That's a great idea!" Ariel bolted for the kitchen.

"I'm kind of tired," Miranda said. "I'm going to bed."

"Go ahead, honey." Richard sat on the couch, and Skip sat next to him, resting one protective arm behind his friend's back. Miranda wondered if this was all an act. She wondered what would have been happening right now if Adam hadn't stayed in the hospital. Something like Little Bighorn, maybe.

"Good night." She left the room feeling defeated.

"God!" she heard Skip say. "When I first looked at her, I thought it was Jasmine's ghost."

"I never think about that," Richard said. "Miranda's so different from her, I never think about the likeness."

Miranda had stopped and was eavesdropping. *What does that mean? How am I different from my mother?*

"What did the doctor say?" Skip asked.

Miranda didn't want to hear all that again.

"Look what I found!" Ariel called. Apparently it was some kind of good liquor.

"Atta girl!" said Skip. "I knew I liked you."

Miranda went into her room and closed the door. She stared at her image in the wall mirror. It looked like a skinny, hostile boy looking back. She couldn't imagine her wild, beautiful, Gypsy mother resembling that. Miranda focused on the eyes. Maybe with makeup they would be striking. Lila had said Miranda had her mother's eyes. That must mean Jasmine's eyes were brown, too.

But somehow Miranda knew it was the wrong answer. She knew her mother's eyes hadn't been brown.

Was that a memory? Knowing what something was not?

Miranda raised her window and inhaled the salty,

marshy fragrance. If anything did happen to Lila, that guy in the living room, whose laugh was echoing all the way down the hall, was going to kill everything that lived in the marsh. And maybe make boots out of some of them.

The wind surged and hissed in the dry grasses. The tree frogs picked up and echoed each other's cries like a roomful of panicky children.

eight

Miranda woke up. The moon had risen, spilling harsh light across her bed. She vaguely felt she had heard a cry from the marsh, but she wasn't sure. Her back felt tense and full of energy. Something in her wanted to get up. And walk.

She thought of Adam at the hospital. She could picture him, lying on that couch in the waiting area outside the coronary care unit. She saw him on his side, one of his arms hanging down, fingers brushing the carpet. His hair covered his face like a black silk curtain. All these details were vivid in her mind. She could see the squarish fluorescent light above him and a crushed watercooler cup on the floor near his fingers. She even thought she heard a vacuum cleaner droning in the background.

Stop it. This is weird. She sat up to dispel the image. Then she felt regretful. Maybe it had been some kind of magic, like a mental connection between her and Adam. Maybe in his dreaming, he had reached out to her and let her see the hospital. Maybe she could have gone on to Lila's room and checked on her.

Thinking of Lila brought Miranda down. Her chest felt heavy and hollow at the same time.

The cry sounded again. It was a strange, flutelike sound, like a bird, only dry and more melodious. Maybe like the wind blowing through a reed just the right way. Although the sound was sweet, it made Miranda shiver. She went to the window to listen.

The moon cut a silver path through the saw grass and drew squiggly lines in the black estuaries. The songs of frogs, crickets and cicadas meshed in a rhythm like machinery. An alligator grunted. But the cry did not repeat.

Miranda's fingers tightened on the windowsill. She tried to resist what she was feeling. She had a powerful urge to walk in the marsh. It wasn't like a feeling inside her. It was like something out there, calling her. She closed the window and looked around for some clothes.

The night air made Miranda shiver, which was strange because the day had been hot. The wind seemed to come and go in teasing gusts. Miranda touched the picnic table as she passed it and ducked under the bird feeders. Slowly she began to pick her way down the silver footpath into the marsh.

The chorus of grunts, clicks, taps and croaks grew louder with every step. She walked with her arms folded against her body for warmth. Were alligators nocturnal? she wondered. She knew that by day they were sluggish and avoided people, but what about at night? What about bears, bobcats? Adam had told her there were even a few panthers in the wetlands. Miranda had the feeling of stepping on someone else's turf, at a time when they had all the advantages.

And she didn't even know why she was doing this. Her grandmother was in the hospital fighting for her life. Miranda should be resting, getting ready to face whatever would happen at the hospital tomorrow. But the urge to walk forward was as irresistible as a hot fudge sundae.

Matted grass squished under Miranda's sneakers. The cry sounded again. Miranda froze and turned in its direction, waiting. Wind rattled the saw grass. "Hello?" Miranda rasped. "Is anyone there?"

A bush nearby became agitated, and two little red eyes peered out at Miranda before the small, ratlike creature jumped out of the bush and dove in the water. She waited for her startle reaction to pass, then walked on in the direction of the cry.

She noticed a heavy, sweet scent in the air. It might be jasmine, Miranda thought. She had been interested in jasmine all her life because it was her mother's name. She knew it grew wild in Florida and released its scent at night. But this was a richer, spicier scent, familiar—it was a lot like her grandmother's white ginger cologne.

The cry came again, this time very close. Miranda stood still, holding her breath, scanning the twisted Halloween shapes of cypress trees, the circular waves of wind in the saw grass, the harsh, moonlit water.

Something made her look over her left shoulder. Perched on the low branches of a mangrove tree was a grackle. The moonlight brought out a fiery turquoise in his black feathers. His eyes were like gold lasers. He stared at Miranda hard, then tipped his head back and repeated the fluty cry.

Miranda felt a cold paralysis. Unable to take her eyes off the bird, she stumbled backward in fear. *Birds don't come out at night.*

She clearly remembered the birthday party of a friend when she was six years old, the fun demonstration with the parakeet in the cage. Cover it up, the bird slipped into unconsciousness; shine a light, the bird woke up. Except for owls, they were all that way as far as Miranda knew. This bird couldn't, shouldn't, wouldn't be here, staring and singing to Miranda.

The grackle cocked his head and piped again. The cry was almost physically seductive. Miranda thought she was almost feeling it in her body more than hearing it. "I'm dreaming," she told the bird. "Because you can't be here."

Or maybe there was a rational explanation. Maybe bright moonlight could wake a bird up, fool him into thinking it was daytime. Miranda wanted to think carefully so that she wouldn't hear the voice in the back of her brain telling her this was a magical bird that had called her here.

"Tell me what you want," Miranda said, hearing the edges of fear poking through her voice. If only Adam had been there, he could have guided her through this experience—whether it was natural . . . or not.

The bird fastidiously readjusted his feet so that his body squarely faced Miranda. He stared at her piercingly.

"Are you the bird I tried to feed?" she pleaded. "Are you the bird who came to my window?"

He continued to stare.

Something trembled inside Miranda—a future sob gathering energy. "Did you come to tell me Lila's dead?"

The bird slowly lowered his head, then raised it

121

again, looking Miranda square in the eye. Her body jolted again. Had he nodded, *yes?* Abruptly he spread his wings and flew away, his silhouette crossing the moon before the dark sky swallowed him.

"No!" Miranda called. "Please don't go! Please!" The sob rose to her throat and choked her. She knelt in the wet grass, feeling it soak into her sweatpants. She pulled up handfuls of grass and weeds and inhaled their scent as she cried.

When Miranda staggered in the kitchen door, her father was already on the telephone. His fingers were white-tight on the receiver. Tears stood in the corners of his eyes. "Wait a minute," he said. He covered the mouthpiece and looked at Miranda. "Where have you been? You're all dirty."

Miranda realized little bits of the marsh were dropping off her onto the kitchen floor. "Is that the doctor?" she asked.

"Yes." Richard's voice cracked. "She's . . ."

"I know." Miranda leaned against the sink, not sure whether she wanted to wash her hands or throw up.

"Go get Ariel," he said, then spoke into the receiver again. "Yes, I'm here, I'm sorry. Should I come down now?"

Miranda turned on the tap and put her hands under scalding water. "I want to go, too."

He shook his head, but Miranda decided she was going no matter what he said. She dried her hands on a paper towel and went to the guest room. "Ariel?" she called from the doorway. "Grandma's dead. She died."

Ariel sat up, sweeping her hair back with one hand. "What?"

Miranda sagged against the door frame. "Grandma died. She just died. She's dead. Grandma's dead." *Shut up, you sound like you're going crazy.* Miranda stared at the floor, feeling paralyzed. She heard the rustling of Ariel getting up and then felt herself in a warm tangle of arms and nightgown and hair. She swayed on her feet.

"Hey," Ariel said. "Do you want to sit down? Where's Rich? What's going on?"

"I'm okay." Miranda pushed her stepmother away and slid toward the bed, managing to sit just before her knees buckled. "Dad's in the kitchen. On the phone to the doctor."

Ariel rushed off. Miranda toppled on her side and pulled her knees up for her second wave of crying. All she could think of was Adam—how she wanted to reach for him right now, the way a scared baby reaches for a blanket.

The hospital lights were harsh after the silent, dark car ride. Everything like that, every noise or shift in temperature, made Miranda jump. It was as if she were asleep and things kept waking her up.

They met Dr. Suzuki outside the patient room where Lila had been moved. The doctor had red eyes, just like the family. "I'm so sorry, Dr. Gates," he said to Richard. "Lila was one of my favorite patients. She was so . . ." He looked all around the ceiling for a word but couldn't find one. "I've been here since one. I came as soon as she went into cardiac arrest. We tried everything, but her heart just wouldn't cooperate." He put a hand on Richard's arm, and Richard reached up and touched it.

"Thank you, Doctor. I know you did everything you could."

Dr. Suzuki sighed.

"She's"—Richard pointed to the doorway of the room—"in there?"

"Yes. Adam's with her. He hasn't left her side. I'll sign the death certificate unless you want an autopsy for any reason, but I think . . ."

"Obviously, yes." Richard had his head down. "We know the cause of death."

"If you know which funeral home you want, I can make the call for you."

Richard looked up. "You're being very kind, Doctor, but there's nothing else you can do. We'll take over from here. Frankly, you look like you need some rest."

"Yeah." Dr. Suzuki sighed, looked at the doorway of the room one more time and trudged away, touching Miranda gently as he passed her.

They all watched him walk down the corridor and disappear. "He's a good guy," Richard said. Miranda thought they were all stalling a little. She'd never seen a dead person except on the evening news, and they were usually all covered up. And strangers. This was going to be Lila. Dead. Lila, dead; Lila, dead. Part of Miranda refused to put the two concepts together.

Her father was touching her. "Do you want to stay out here? You don't have to . . ."

"No." Miranda shook her head. "Adam's been alone with her. I want to go in."

"Okay." He touched her shoulder, steering her gently through the half-curtained doorway. Ariel trailed them.

Miranda saw things in slow motion at first. The light seemed dim and fuzzy. Adam sat on a stool by the bed, holding Lila's hand. *Holding her hand.*

Lila looked small. Miranda had known she was short, but something about her vitality had made her seem big and strong, and now she was a tiny old woman. Her rosy complexion was gray. Her blue eyes were closed.

All her colors were gone. Her features had turned brittle and sharp. Her feet only came halfway down the length of the bed. In a weird contrast, her hair was unpinned and fell over the pillow in shiny white waves. It was as if all the life in her had come out the top of her head. Miranda saw all this in one long, horrible second, while two voices screeched in her head. One was screaming, *Grandma.* The other was screaming, *Corpse.* Miranda began to cry, a choppy sobbing that was almost like hiccups.

Adam let go of Lila's hand—was it cold?—stood and opened his arms to Miranda. She gratefully lunged into the warmth, resting her ear against his beating heart.

Faintly, she was aware that her father had brushed by them and picked up the telephone.

He talked to the funeral home for a minute and hung up. Miranda let go of Adam and stared at Lila. What would happen now? Were they coming with a van or something to carry Lila away? Was Lila's body a thing now? Where was the rest of her?

"What are you going to do?" The words were so sharp and fierce, they shattered Miranda's thoughts. She looked at Adam, who was glaring at Richard, challenging him.

"What?" Richard looked exhausted, distracted.

"She's dead. She can't defend her property anymore,

man. What are you going to do?" Adam's brown eyes looked red in this light.

Richard rubbed his eyes. "Adam, please, not tonight. Don't you realize?"

"That's what she'd want to know," Adam said. "I'm asking for her."

"Adam, we're all suffering," Richard said softly. "This is an ordeal for all of us. The easiest way to release tension is to turn on each other, but—"

"Don't shrink me, mister!" Adam's voice was almost a growl. Miranda stepped back from him. "Answer me. You know what you're going to do. Can you really violate your mother's wishes? I want you to tell me while she's still in this room and you have to look at her!"

"Shut uuuuuup!" Richard's scream was almost unearthly, and his body launched at Adam.

"No!" Ariel cried as Richard's hands clamped like claws on Adam's shoulders. "Rich!"

Adam, in turn, clamped his hands on Richard's shoulders. Miranda opened her mouth to scream, but nothing came out. Somehow Adam swung or shoved Richard away from him. Richard slammed shoulder-first into a wall. He stared at Adam, panting.

"I don't let anybody lay their hands on me like that!" Adam shouted. "Not anyone!"

Richard's voice was both raging and tearful. He touched his shoulder. "My-mother-is-dead!" The words came out like little gunshots. "My mother! *My* mother! Get it? I don't care about wills and property. All I can think about is my mother, whom I have just lost! Okay?"

Adam ducked his head. "Look, I'm—"

"Shut up. I mean it. And get out of here. You're not a member of my family and you never will be. And I want you out of here right now."

Adam bit his lip. "Look, I'm sorry. I—"

Richard's eyes showed white all around the iris. "Shut up! And if you don't get out of here now, I'll call Security and have you thrown out. And you'd better make plans to move off *my* property."

Adam stared at Richard for several long seconds. Then he lowered his head and took off.

"And you keep away from my daughter, too!" Richard shouted. Then he sagged against the wall. "Damn him."

Ariel reached for him. "It's okay, Rich. Calm down."

Miranda kept staring at the door Adam had gone through. It was all she could do not to run after him.

Instead she turned and looked at her grandmother again. In her mind, Miranda saw Lila at the dinner table, raising a wineglass, teasing and laughing. It seemed as if Lila had been holding so many things together. The family, her house, the marsh and all the animals in it. Now the pieces were flying in every direction. There was a war, and people were choosing up sides.

And Miranda didn't know which side she was on.

nine

"Miranda?" Ariel called from her room. "Could you come here for a second?"

Miranda sat at her window, gazing at a mist that blanketed the marsh. The birds made a racket this morning—there must have been a cat or snake on the trails.

Miranda had been sitting there for twenty minutes with one sock on and one in her hand, trying to summon the energy to finish dressing for the funeral.

"Miranda? Are you there?"

"What do you want!" Grief, for Miranda, seemed to be like a raging case of PMS. She'd been taking out her frustration on everyone for days.

Ariel's voice became small, girlish. "I really need your help, honey."

Miranda threw her sock across the room and kicked her shoes out of the way with a clatter. She marched over to the other guest room. "What!" she said again.

Ariel was standing over the bed in a black slip that splayed dramatically above and below her narrow waist. Her hair was all pulled to one side, spilling over her shoulder. *What is Daryl Hannah doing at my grandmother's funeral?* Miranda thought bitterly.

"What am I going to do?" Ariel swept her hand across a display of black dresses laid out on the bed. One had spaghetti straps. One had a plunging neckline. One had a short full skirt like a French maid's uniform and a sash printed with scarlet roses. One was backless with a black velvet bow over the butt.

"What am I going to do?" Ariel moaned. "I've never been to a funeral in my life. My whole family are healthy as horses! When I buy a black dress, it's—"

"Wear a different color," Miranda said. "Wear your white suit."

"I didn't bring it! We were coming to Florida for a goddamned vacation, not some—"

"Ari, I don't even have a dress. I'm wearing pants because that's all I have. Are we going to get mad at my grandmother for dying and screwing up our packing strategy?" Miranda felt her face burn, but she didn't know if it was anger or shame.

Maybe shame. Ariel froze as if she'd been slapped. Then all the air seemed to go out of her. She sat on the bed, crushing the dress pile. Her head slowly tilted forward, and a curtain of hair closed her off from view. "No, honey, that's not what I meant. I meant I know I'm going to let Richard down as a wife because I only know how to be a girlfriend."

Miranda was afraid the next thing would be tears, but instead, nothing happened. Ariel sat slumped, like a puppet with the strings cut.

The last thing Miranda wanted to see was another woman with the life draining out of her. "Ari?" She stepped closer but kept her arms folded. "I'm really sorry. I'm so sad right now I don't know what I'm saying. I screamed at Daddy this morning just because he had to be at the funeral home early . . . I can't seem to talk to Adam at all . . . we're all screwed up. I'm still your friend."

The hair curtain swung as Ariel nodded. Miranda knew it wasn't enough. Much as she hated the idea, she realized that right at that moment, Ariel was in more pain than she was.

Miranda took another step, which put her beside the bed. She lifted a strand of blond hair and tugged it gently. "What's going on in there?"

Ariel threw her head back, inhaling sharply. Her eyes were red, as if she'd been crying, but there were no tears. "What am I doing here, Miranda?" she asked in a monotone. "Do I look like I belong here? Why did your dad marry me, anyway? What was he thinking?"

"He told me it was because he loved you," Miranda said.

"Well," Ariel said, her voice trembling, "that was a lie, Miranda. How can you love somebody when you don't know them? This"—she gestured all around—"is your father. Florida and his mother and the swamp and the birds and . . . you. And your mother. When he married me I think he was trying to get away from all that. I'm some fantasy he had in junior high when he was listening to a Beach Boys album."

"No, Ari, you're selling yourself way short."

"I'm tired of not fitting into his world. It makes me sell myself short. I like who I am, but does he?"

"Ari, we were talking about how you don't have a funeral dress. Now you're getting all complicated."

"Okay, I'll make it easier." Ariel's jaw was so tense, her hair trembled. "I don't know what Rich is thinking, but I know what I've been thinking, and he's not what I wanted. I think I made a terrible mistake!" Finally she cried for real, slumping again, cupping her hands to her face, her back heaving.

Miranda sat beside her. She felt panicky—was everyone leaving at once? "You don't even know what you're saying. It's the funeral and everything. You're blowing things up bigger than they are." She patted her stepmother's shaking back, trying at the same time to keep her fingers from getting caught in the tangled hair. "And you're wrong that you don't fit in here. I think in some ways you're a lot like Lila."

This was apparently so shocking to Ariel, she abruptly stopped crying. "Like what?"

"Go look in *her* closet! I'll bet you'll find the same five dresses in there somewhere!"

Ariel laughed, brushing away tears with the back of her hand.

"Ari, she's being buried in that horrible orange dress with the flamenco ruffles on the skirt. What does that tell you? If you wear a sexy dress to her funeral, it will be like a tribute!"

Ariel pulled a tissue from the box on the nightstand, blew her nose and stood up. "Well," she said, studying the dress pile, "which one of these babies do you think Lila would like most?"

Miranda leaned over and smoothed them. "The red sash, definitely."

It was windy at the cemetery. Miranda felt her thoughts scattering and swooping like the yellow leaves falling from the ash trees that surrounded them. She looked at Adam, hardly recognizing him. Not only was he wearing a suit and tie, but he had shown up with his hair cut short. As Miranda had sputtered and choked, he'd explained it was a Native American form of mourning—a sacrifice to honor the dead person and a symbol of how long the grieving process would take. Any other time, Miranda would have been impressed, but the loss of Adam's beautiful hair was almost like another death for her—one too many. She hadn't said anything, but now she kept sneaking glances at this stranger he'd become—a sharp-featured Latin American attorney, not the eighteen-year-old "yard boy" who had kissed her on the beach. There was something else weird about him as he stood there, dappled with sun and shade, something that made him look different from everyone else at the funeral. After a while, Miranda realized he was the only one standing absolutely still.

"I've officiated at over a hundred funerals," the priest was saying. The priest had been another surprise—a short, red-haired woman who walked with a limp and told the family to call her Sandy. "For me, the hardest part of a funeral is when they lower the coffin into the ground. That air of finality. It's often the moment when the family really cries and releases their grief." Sandy paused to pull a wisp of hair out of her mouth. "But I don't think I'm going to feel like that today. And all of you who knew Lila, will know why." Sandy paused for effect, looking at each of them in turn. Then she pointed to the ground. "This is Lila's favorite place." Her voice was full of wonder, like the story lady at the library. "This is the earth. This is the place Lila dedicated her life to, the place she cared so deeply about. This is her true home."

Weeping broke out from a cluster of older ladies Miranda didn't know. She assumed they were fellow conservationists because they had been bird-watching before the service started. They wore a fascinating array of outfits, everything from a lavender "church" dress to an oversized T-shirt with a picture of a wolf. One of them had a gigantic straw cartwheel of a hat, lemon yellow with a turquoise ribbon. Miranda wished it was appropriate to take pictures at a funeral.

"Lila came to my church after her first heart attack," Sandy went on. "She told me she thought she was a pagan."

There was a soft ripple of sad laughter.

"She told me she frankly had no use for my religion at all. She said she thought the only thing Episcopalians worshipped was golf scores."

Miranda heard her father's laughter above the others.

"However. Lila told me that any religion that has women priests can't be all bad. And then she proceeded

to tell me how she wanted this ceremony to be con-
ducted."

Miranda studied the small triangle formed by Skip
Wilson, her father and Ariel. Skip stood behind them,
towering over them. Was he looking down Ariel's
dress? *No, even he wouldn't sink that low,* Miranda
thought. Ariel had put a wide ribbon around her hair to
keep it from blowing in the wind. That, plus the sash,
made her look like a sexy Alice in Wonderland. She
hugged herself, maybe trying to cover the sash with her
arms.

"Lila wanted me to comfort all of you, rather than
talk about her," Sandy was saying. "She asked me to
remind you that death is an essential part of nature—
and that if you truly love the earth and its processes,
then you must accept death, too."

The environmental ladies murmured assent.

Sandy hooked her hair behind her ear. "She wanted
me to tell you that if you love her, if you want to do
something to remember her, do something for the
causes she believed in. Do something to help the wild
things she loved."

Miranda looked at her father. Tears stood in his eyes.
Ariel was looking at him, too. Skip Wilson rolled his
eyes.

"Apparently, in the last year of her life, Lila was exposed to some Native American philosophy." Sandy smiled at Adam. He ducked his head. "Lila told me her favorite concept was the phrase *all my relations*. When Indians pray, they pray for the animals and plants, the rocks, the elements, even the earth itself, and they refer to them with this phrase: *All my relations*."

One of the older ladies sighed.

Sandy touched her heart. "In my Episcopal language, that says to me that this is a woman who loved all of creation. And therefore a woman who truly loved God. Lila was a person who was glad to be alive and part of this world. Her life had beauty and meaning because she knew who she was and where she belonged. She wanted a graveside service because her funeral had to be outdoors." Sandy gestured to the woods that surrounded them. "So that all her relations could attend."

Miranda bowed her head to accommodate a sudden rush of tears.

"So, in closing, I'll address this to all of Lila's relations. Let's take a moment to remember her."

Crying quietly, Miranda listened to the sounds of wind and birds around her. She realized what Lila had meant to her. She would never look at or listen to the world in the same way again.

When they lowered the coffin, Miranda's father threw in a handful of dirt. Adam stepped forward and tossed in a sprig of wild thyme. The ash tree contributed a handful of yellow leaves.

After the service, Skip Wilson came back to Lila's house with them. Adam retreated to his own house without a word. Ariel went to change, and Richard went straight to the refrigerator, getting a beer for himself and one for Skip, who was sprawled all over Lila's little divan.

Miranda felt her anger bubbling up. This was not the place she wanted to be. She wished she could be with the ladies, who had probably gone straight out to plant a tree in Lila's name. Or Adam. Maybe he was doing a little ceremony of his own. Even Sandy, who didn't know them, seemed more moved than the family.

Skip looked as if he were waiting for a tailgate party to start. Miranda thought maybe she would just leave right now and go over to Adam's to show, once and for all, what side she was on. But then she realized she wanted to stay and hear what was said. She also realized that made her a spy.

"Can I have a beer, too, Daddy?" she called, to position herself as an innocuous teenager with no agenda.

Richard came in and handed a beer to Skip, then popped his own. "I don't think so, sweetheart. I only let you drink that wine because Mom was insisting and I didn't want to fight with her. But I don't want you to think you should take a drink when you're feeling bad."

And your example here won't affect me at all.

Ariel came out in jeans and a T-shirt, combing her fingers through her hair.

"Hey!" Skip said. "Who told you you could take off that dynamite dress?"

Ariel frowned at him, then turned to Richard. "I wish I'd had time to shop for something more appropriate."

He waved his hand. "It isn't important."

Ariel studied him for a minute. "Beer!" she said finally. "What a great idea. We ought to have a wake and get roaring drunk!"

"I'm in," Skip said. He turned to Richard. "Did you get a load of those hat ladies? Chee! They made Lila look conservative! How many of them do you figure—"

"Hey, do you mind?" Richard interrupted him. "Those were my mother's friends."

"Whoops! Sorry! Really, Rich, I'm just trying to lighten the mood. I know this whole thing is hard on you. I mean did you catch the infomercial for conservation Lila slipped in there? You're the relation she was trying to convert."

Ariel returned from the kitchen and perched on the arm of the couch. Richard didn't answer Skip and looked very spacy. "Drink your beer, honey," Ariel said. "It's dripping sweat onto your shoes."

Richard obediently tipped the beer up and took five or six long swallows.

Miranda looked away.

"So what's next?" Skip asked, sitting up and putting his feet on the floor. "You gonna meet with her attorney?"

Miranda had to restrain herself not to jump on him like a guard dog.

Richard answered in a neutral voice. "I called her lawyer yesterday. She left a videotape will. Obviously, she's put a whole lot of planning into all this. He's coming to play it for us on Thursday."

"You want me to be here?" Skip asked. His face was a bad parody of friendly concern. Miranda pictured herself taking the beer from his hand and pouring it over his head. Why was her father so taken in by this clown?

"No," Richard answered. "This is a family thing. I'll call you Friday."

Miranda couldn't hold it any longer. "Why?"

Richard blinked at her. "Why what?"

"Why would you call him Friday? Why does he get a call right after you inherit? Are you going to sell Grandma out the very next day?"

There was a long silence, and Miranda realized all the adults were staring at her, as if she'd pulled a knife on them.

"Miranda, honey," Richard said. "This is hard enough for me. Are you trying to make it worse?"

"Make what worse?" Miranda cried. "Are you too chicken to say what you're going to do?"

Ariel touched Richard's shoulder as if she thought Miranda was abusing him.

"I don't know what I'm going to do, okay?" Richard snapped at his daughter.

"You don't?" Skip inquired.

Richard's face was red. He glared at Skip. "No, I don't. And I don't appreciate all the lobbying from both sides!" He swung his glare to Miranda. "Especially at a time when all I want to do is grieve for my goddamned mother! Okay?" He was shouting at Miranda.

"Okay!" she said.

"Okay?" he yelled at Skip.

"Okay!"

"Okay!" Ariel said to make them laugh. The laugh was nervous and followed by a stifling silence.

"I'm going for a walk," Miranda said, getting up.

"I'm ready for another round," Ariel said. "Anybody joining me?"

"Yes!" said the two men together.

As soon as Miranda knocked, Adam said, "Come in."

He sat on the bed with his hands folded, staring at the

142

rug. His face still looked alien to Miranda without the frame of hair around it.

"I can't get used to the way you look," she blurted out.

"It'll grow back," he said listlessly.

"What's going on over there? Are they having Lila's furniture appraised?"

Miranda sat on the bed next to him. She figured it was safe to do since they were both depressed out of their minds. "No. They're getting drunk."

Adam made a noise of contempt. "Figures. I guess I should be getting ready for my eviction notice."

Miranda hadn't even thought of that. "There's a videotaped will," she said. "The lawyer is coming to play it on Thursday."

"I know," he said. "I'm invited."

"You are?"

"Well, sure!" He looked up. "We were really close friends!"

"I'm sorry," Miranda said. "I know you were. She's probably going to leave you all those bird feeders!"

"I'd like the bird feeders!" he said. "They're great bird feeders!"

Miranda leaned against his shoulder because she felt like it. "What did you think of the funeral?"

Adam smiled. "That lady was good. The only thing better would have been a pagan ceremony out on the marsh in the moonlight with everybody dancing and shaking rattles—but I can't see your dad doing that."

Miranda was laughing hard. "I can't, either. But, Adam?"

"What?"

"We could do that."

"Do what?"

"Go out in the marsh and have our own ceremony for Lila."

He laughed. "Okay. Let's see, we'll get naked and start dancing . . ."

She smacked him gently. "I didn't say that. But something Grandma would like. Do you know anything about Native American funerals?"

He shrugged. "Different groups do different things. But I think people should make up their own ceremonies from things that are meaningful to them."

Immediately Miranda had an idea. "I want to paint my face."

"Get out!"

"I do. I remember what you told me. That some Indians put paint on their faces so the spirits could see them? I want to paint my face so Grandma can see me, and then I'll promise to do something for her causes, like she asked."

"That's pretty cool," Adam said. "I think I could get into that."

144

"We could use her lipstick!"

"Oh, whoa. Step off. I'll come up with my own idea."

"Whatever. When can we do it?"

"Friday night?"

"It's a date. We meet in the marsh at midnight for a pagan funeral."

Adam grinned. "Much more creative than a movie date."

Miranda laughed and threw her arms around him. "Oh, I love you!" she said. Then she heard the words and pulled back. "I didn't mean to say that!"

His grin, if anything, had gotten bigger. "Maybe you didn't mean to," he said, "but you did."

ten

Lila's lawyer looked younger than Adam. He parted his hair in the middle and wore little round glasses. His name was Benedict Blount.

He spent about a half hour on his hands and knees, making sure he could work Lila's VCR. Since he didn't want to give away any secrets of the will, Benedict Blount had asked for a different videotape to practice on. Adam brought out Lila's favorite movie, *The Wizard of Oz*.

Miranda thought back to Lila's heart attack, how she'd been singing "Over the Rainbow" as she strolled through the marsh. Miranda realized she'd taken pictures of her grandmother that day! The film was still in the camera. As soon as this was over, she would fire off the rest of the shots and take the film to the drugstore. She'd ask Adam to go with her. They'd probably both need some cheering up after this ordeal.

Right now Adam was looking down at his lap, not making eye contact with Miranda or anyone. He had pulled a straight chair in from the dining room, even though there was plenty of living room furniture. Miranda couldn't tell if his silence was grief or sullenness.

Richard and Ariel sat on the couch together, holding hands. Richard was frowning at Benedict Blount's incompetence. Ariel seemed to be studying the seat of the lawyer's pants as he crawled back and forth, squinting at buttons. Miranda knew that early this morning, Ariel had put a shot of vodka in her coffee. One more thing to worry about.

The other person in the room was one of the hat ladies from the funeral, whose name, they now knew, was Evelina Lincoln-Whitt. She was president of the Florida Friends of the Wetlands. It figured she might be getting a sizable donation. Miranda wondered if Lila had left all her property to one of those organizations and beat Skip Wilson that way. Evelina Lincoln-Whitt wore a magenta suit of boiled wool, accented with a gigantic brooch of synthetic pink crystals. She looked as impatient with Benedict Blount as Richard was.

"Maybe I could help you with something," Richard said, leaning forward.

"No, no, I'm getting it," Blount said cheerfully. He hit a button. Judy Garland disappeared and was replaced by the Weather Channel. "Okay, that's definitely wrong," he muttered to himself.

Richard dropped Ariel's hand and half stood. "Look, you had it. Just make sure it's rewound, press Play, and that's it!"

Benedict Bount turned all the way around and smiled. "It's imperative to get it right, Mr. Gates. You're supposed to see this all the way through without a hitch."

"*Doctor* Gates," Richard muttered.

"Maybe I should go make some coffee," Ariel said.

She wants another shot of vodka, Miranda thought.

"I only drink tea," said Evelina Lincoln-Whitt.

"I don't want anything," Adam said.

Ariel stood up, tugging her dress. "I'll just get myself a glass of water."

Finally Benedict Blount seemed satisfied. He popped out *The Wizard of Oz* and popped in the tape labled *Lila Gates—LWT.* He tapped the Rewind button several times, then turned to his audience. "I want to say a few things. . . . Where is Mrs. Gates?"

"I'm here!" Ariel trotted in, looking flushed. She sat down heavily next to Richard, who glanced at her.

"Before we start," Benedict Blount continued, "I'm sure you know that these taped wills are becoming more

148

common. It's a companion to the written will Lila had drawn on the same date, which you'll all receive a copy of, as well as the tape. This was taped in our office in the presence of witnesses, where we will retain a copy for reference in case of a dispute. I'd just like to warn you that it's often shocking, so soon after the funeral, to watch one of these tapes. Some family members have said it's like seeing the loved one alive again. Don't be surprised if you have an emotional reaction to seeing Lila and hearing her voice. The law requires me to play this tape through once, for all of you, with no pauses or interruptions. So I ask you not to react or leave the room until the whole tape is played. If you do so, we have to start from the beginning. If, after the tape has been played, you have questions or would like portions to be played back to you, I'll be happy to do that. Any questions?"

There were no questions. Miranda caught herself biting a cuticle and put her hands in her lap.

"Okay," said Benedict Blount. "This is it." He tapped the Play button. Lila's face, her soft white hair, her dancing eyes, filled the screen.

"Oh!" Miranda cried, and then clapped her hand over her mouth.

Lila sat at a table, presumably in the law office. A shelf of artificial-looking books stood behind her. Her hands were folded on the table like those of a schoolgirl.

She wore a white blouse with a frill at the neck, the most conservative thing Miranda had ever seen her wear. Her eyes seemed so blue and her cheeks so pink . . . Miranda realized she was comparing this image to the corpse.

"Well, I hardly know how to begin!" Lila said. "I mean, after all, I'm dead and you're grieving. It hardly seems like a time for pleasantries!"

Everyone laughed nervously except Adam. Ariel laughed a little too loudly.

"But I want to say something personal to you before we get right down to business. Each and every one of you. I'm taping this in May. A year ago February I had a heart attack. The doctors tell me I don't have a dependable heartbeat anymore. I've reached the point in my life where I have to get serious and face some things I haven't wanted to face. I know I'm going to die someday. Maybe soon. When I do, I want to have an easy mind. I want to know all my unfinished business is finished. And the biggest item I have on that list is you, Richie."

Miranda, and everyone else, turned to Richard, who flinched and then blushed. It reminded Miranda of those scenes in murder mysteries where the detective gathers the suspects together and points to each of them in turn.

"Richie, when I finish this recording, I'm going to

pick up the phone and call you. It's been ten years, and I think we both know this is ridiculous. I'm angry with you even as I record this, and you know why I'm angry, but you're also my son, Richard. I've always loved you and been tremendously proud of you."

Richard hunched forward and began to cry silently. Ariel put her arm around him.

"So I'm going to call you and hope you'll bring Miranda and your new wife down to Florida for the summer and see if we can pick up where we left off and maybe this time sort the issues out. I don't think I have much time anymore, which makes me look at everything differently. If this visit doesn't happen, Richard, I want you to know that reconciliation was my intention. I wanted to resolve things between us because you're the most important person in the world to me."

A sound, almost like a moan, came out of Miranda's father. Ariel pulled him closer.

"I can't say anything personal to you, Ariel, because I haven't met you. I hope by now you haven't decided I'm a horrible mother-in-law. I was so glad to get your wedding announcement. Richard has a very morbid disposition and he needs someone fun to give him perspective. Jasmine was like that, and when I saw your photograph and that big smile, I thought, *Richard made a good choice.*"

"Oh, god," Ariel whispered.

"Miranda, you're another reason I realized I had to come down off my high horse and make peace with your father. We don't even know each other. I don't know what kind of girl you are—your pictures give nothing away—and I wanted you to know me before it was too late. I want you to see my home and the marsh and my animals and birds—that's what I am. I hope by now we've met and hit it off and become friends—"

"Oh, yes!" Miranda said.

"—and I'm sorry my pigheadedness kept you from seeing me while you were growing up. In case you have come to like me and you're missing me now, I have some advice for you. If you feel bad, go and take a walk in the marsh among the wild things. That's where you'll find me. That's where you'll always find me."

Miranda bit her lip. A sound came out of her, almost identical to her father's moan, only an octave higher.

"Evelina, you're my dearest friend on earth."

Miranda looked up through her tears at Evelina, who stared at the screen stone-faced, one of those people, Miranda thought, who freeze when they feel emotion.

Lila was smiling warmly at the camera, and therefore at Evelina. "We fought some great battles together, didn't we, dear? Remember the sea turtles? And that ridiculous bill in the state legislature on dolphin feeding? I think, even though our victories were small, we'll be leaving the world a little better than we found it. And we really had fun along the way, didn't we?"

Evelina mouthed the word *yes* without making any sound.

"And then there's you, Adam," Lila was saying. "An unexpected gift, to use your favorite word. Just when I was too frail to hold on to my home by myself, there you were with all the strength I needed. How do you suppose it happened, that this old lady found her soul mate so late in life and that he turned out to be a raggedy runaway teenager? I know we both believe in fate, Adam, and obviously we were meant to meet and help each other."

Adam turned his face away from the screen and everyone in the room.

"Well! Enough of this sugary slop!" Lila slapped her hands on the table. "I guess you'd all like to hear about the money." She looked at someone off camera and giggled. "All right, here goes. One hundred thousand dollars in trust to Miranda for college or for the educational experience of her choice. Meaning, dear, if you don't want to go to college, you can run off to Italy and study puppetry, or whatever takes your fancy. Use the money to make a dream come true for yourself, that's all I ask. One hundred thousand dollars donated to the Friends of the Wetlands in your name, Evelina."

"Oh!" Evelina touched her heart.

"You can buy a lot of nesting grounds for that kind of money!" Lila went on. She seemed almost giddy from the fun of giving her money away. "And for you personally, Evelina, you can take anything you'd like from my home, clothing, art, jewelry, whatever, before it becomes part of the estate. Don't be cheap with yourself, take something nice or take as many things as you want. I want you to have a beautiful remembrance of me."

Miranda looked at Evelina. She was still composed, but tears stood in her eyes.

"One hundred thousand dollars to you, Richard, and . . ." Lila took a deep breath. "The rest of the estate, my house, my land, and all the remaining cash assets, which they tell me is a little short of a million, to you, Adam."

Miranda thought at first she had heard wrong. But hearing the word *What?* explode out of her father told her she hadn't.

"Mr. Gates, we can't stop the tape," Benedict Blount cautioned. "Please wait."

"I know you'll be angry, Richard, and hurt. But what else could I do? I simply couldn't trust you with my most important possession."

Miranda's stomach was churning. She looked at Adam, who stared at the screen.

"You bastard!" Richard shouted.

Adam turned around, surprised.

"Please, I have to insist!" Benedict Blount said.

"That marsh is my life, Richard. It's all my life ever stood for. Presiding over a few dumb little birds' nests. Well, for me, that was as important as anything in the world, more important than Skip Wilson's idea of progress, certainly."

"You scheming, plotting—"

"Please!" Benedict Blount's hand hovered over the Pause button.

"You never let me feel safe, Richard. I thought your loyalty was stronger to Skip than it was to me. I hope if I see you this summer, I'll realize that in the end, you'd come down on the right side, and then I'll change this tape and you'll never see it, but as it stands now, I couldn't rest in peace, leaving my property to you."

"Hear, hear!" cried Evelina Lincoln-Whitt.

"You shut up!" Richard sputtered.

"I will not!"

Adam was watching all this as if it had nothing to do with him.

"Please!" said Benedict Blount. "You don't want me to have to play it again."

"Adam understands my land, and he understands me. He'll take good care of things for me. And he needs the money in case there are legal battles he'll have to fight and for maintenance of the house and the marsh. If you don't understand, Richard, I'm sorry. I know it won't be the first time I've let you down as a mother, but at least it's the last."

"How could you!" Richard shouted at the television.

"Well." Lila glanced off screen again. "I guess that's all unless there's some legal mumbo jumbo I have to say to make it stick. No? Well then, good-bye. I hope I haven't started World War Three. Make sure the feeders are full!"

The screen went blank.

Miranda was having trouble thinking straight.

"You knew this, didn't you!" Miranda's father was on his feet, heading toward Adam.

"No, I didn't."

"Liar! You probably planned the whole thing, you little con artist! You probably aren't even a real Indian! Here's my mother, all vulnerable and alone—"

"If you would all just sign this release, I'll be on my way," said Benedict Blount. "It states that you heard the tape and understood—"

"Sign yourself!" Richard yelled.

Miranda noticed that Ariel had gotten up and left the room.

"I didn't scheme anything!" Adam said. "You're the schemer! You and your developer buddy. You heard what she said. She couldn't trust her own son!"

Richard was still closing the distance between them, a

pointing finger extended in front of him. "And you're not her son, and don't you ever forget it. This must be a red-letter day for you, kid. You come out of some holler without a pot to piss in and you find a rich widow and tell her whatever she wants to hear."

"You're tripping!" said Adam.

Evelina Lincoln-Whitt had gone up to the front of the room and signed the release form. "Excuse me," she said to Richard.

"What!"

"When would be a good time for me to come and look through Lila's things? I would like a remembrance or two."

"Well it sure as hell won't be now!" Richard shrieked.

"I'll call tomorrow," she said, "when you're more composed." She gave him the full up-and-down look and then let herself out. At the same time, Miranda heard the back door open and shut. Ariel apparently fleeing.

Adam looked ready to spit. "Look, I don't have to stay here and listen to your abuse." He turned his back to Richard, facing the lawyer. "If I sign that thing I can go, right?"

"Right." Benedict Blount shoved the paper forward eagerly. "And, Mr. Gates, if you and your wife and daughter would sign it, too . . ."

157

"Where's Ariel?" Richard said, looking around.

"I think she took a walk," said Miranda.

"Took a— What the hell is happening around here?"

Adam finished his signature, and Benedict Blount put the paper in his briefcase. "You can sign this later, Mr. Gates, if that's more convenient. I realize that right now you have family issues—"

"It's *Doctor* Gates, and this person is not a member of my family!" Richard shouted.

Miranda felt embarrassed. Her father was practically having a tantrum.

Benedict Blount was headed for the door, zipping his briefcase as he went. "I'll call you in the morning. Good-bye." The door slammed behind him.

Richard and Adam looked at each other. Like killers. Miranda felt sick.

"You get out of here, too," Richard said in a dangerously quiet voice. "Go on back to your hogan and say a prayer to your power animal or whatever it is you do. Unless you don't need that act anymore."

"Daddy . . . ," Miranda said.

Adam held up his hand to Miranda. "Dr. Gates, I'll be happy to go now. But I just want to remind you this is *my* house you're throwing me out of." He turned and walked out, just a trace of shakiness in his steps.

Richard sat down on the couch and began to cry. He took his glasses off and rubbed at his eyes, as if the tears made him angry. "She's my mother, goddammit," he sobbed. "Not his."

Miranda put her hand on his shoulder.

Miranda decided to walk her film to the drugstore alone. She wanted to sort things out, not hear anyone's side for a while.

In a way, she felt sorry for everybody. Her father must be feeling as if his mother had chosen a different son. And Adam must be just as confused. He'd been expecting to inherit a collection of wind chimes and bird feeders, and now he had a house, a huge piece of property, and a bank account he probably couldn't even imagine. This was a long way from that little public-housing shack he'd lived in. A long way from his drunken father in Tennessee.

She knew in the smallest, pettiest part of her, that *she* was annoyed at Adam for getting more than she had. Magnify it a million times for her father. When he was finished crying, Richard had headed straight for his two favorite comforts—a beer from the refrigerator and the portable phone to call Skip Wilson.

That was the only bright spot in this—thinking about Skip Wilson's reaction.

She was not happy to see Adam's old girlfriend, Lindsay Baker, back on duty at the Rexall photo counter.

Today she was wearing a pink T-shirt that said *I'm surrounded by idiots.* She looked prettier than the first time Miranda had seen her. Her brown hair was smooth and shiny, turned under at the ends so that it cupped her chin. She wore rose-colored lipstick and was chewing bubble gum, blowing small, dignified bubbles. Miranda wondered if she and Adam had had sex during their short romance.

"Where's Adam?" Lindsay cocked her head as she passed the processing envelope across the counter to Miranda.

"Back at home," Miranda said.

"I heard about Lila. I'm sorry. She was really nice. Whenever I went over there I'd sit in her kitchen and watch her cook and we'd have these heart-to-heart talks."

Didn't Lila say they just went out once or twice? "I'm writing 'matte finish' on here," Miranda said. "Okay? I don't want to see any gloss."

Lindsay smiled. "I get it. I guess you've already caught on to Adam, huh?"

Miranda looked up from writing. "What do you mean?"

Lindsay blew and popped a cinnamon-scented bubble. "What a liar he is. How you can't trust anything he says. He's a complete con artist with that Indian act. But when I first saw you with him, I knew, even though you were a kid, you were smart enough to figure him out."

Miranda struggled to keep her breathing even. "I have no idea what you mean. Adam has more integrity than anybody I know."

Lindsay laughed. "Okay, fine. My mistake. I just figured by now you'd know he tells everybody what they want to hear. He did that with me and got what he wanted, and then it was good-bye and good luck. Everybody in town used to laugh at how he'd taken Lila in with his little nature-worship show. Well, he got himself a warm dry place to sleep for a while, but I guess he'll have to move on to another meal ticket now."

Miranda's heart was pounding. She struggled to look calm, to keep methodically filling out the envelope.

"Probably next, he'll find a rich Jewish widow and say he's from one of the lost tribes. Here, you have to sign it."

Miranda's signature looked like an old woman's. She left without another word.

"See you!" Lindsay's voice carried after her.

Miranda almost staggered out to the sidewalk.

She realized when he'd left the house today, Adam hadn't even said good-bye to her. In fact, he hadn't really spoken to her at all. Maybe because he didn't need her anymore.

eleven

Skip Wilson came over that night for dinner. Actually, there was no dinner, just a suitcase of Red Wolf beer that Skip brought over. Ariel, who didn't care for beer, had uncorked one of Lila's vintage cabernets. When not in use, it sat like a monument on the coffee table in front of her. No one used glasses. *This is a wake,* Miranda thought, and her next thought was that it was one of the dumber ceremonies mankind had ever come up with. If you're already feeling bad, why do something to make your body feel worse?

Miranda wished someone would offer her a sip.

Instead, they all seemed to have forgotten her. No one mentioned dinner, so she made herself a stack of Ritz cracker-and-peanut-butter sandwiches and wedged herself into a cozy corner on the floor between a lamp and the wall, watching the adults get high.

"To General Custer!" Skip said, lifting his red-and-silver beer can. "Where are you when we need you, man?"

Ariel giggled, then seemed to frown at her own behavior.

Skip placed his hand on her knee, which brought Richard, on her other side, to attention.

Ariel scissored her legs, shaking Skip off. "I don't think we should bring his ethnic background into it," she said, hoisting the bottle.

"I'm convinced he's not really an Indian," Richard said. "Indians happen to be in vogue, and my mother was vulnerable to stuff like that. Two years ago he probably would have said he was an angel. Five years ago, an alien. You know, whatever the flakes are buying that season."

"Don't call Lila a flake!" Miranda cried.

The three of them glanced over as if a loose shutter had rattled, then turned to each other again.

"Well, once the girl is pregnant, there's no point in buying condoms," Skip said.

"I can't follow your crude analogy." Ariel almost seemed to be kissing the neck of the wine bottle.

Richard set his empty on the floor and unhooked a fresh can from the twelve-pack, which Skip was using as a footstool. "There's nothing more to do," said Richard. "It's a legal will. It was my mother's clear intention to screw me, and that's that. Any money I'd spend on lawyers and stuff would be a waste of time."

"I never said a word about lawyers." Skip turned to Ariel. "Did I ever say a word about lawyers?"

The wine sloshed as she set it down. "You didn't say a word about lawyers."

"Okay," Richard said. "So you're talking hit men. Know a good one?"

"Richard . . . Richard . . . You poor naive boy. You wasted so much time getting those college degrees you never learned anything. Lesson one. Everyone has a price."

"I don't think that's true," Miranda said.

This time they didn't even look around.

Richard laughed. "How'm I supposed to bribe the little bastard? He's got my money!"

"I didn't say bribe, I said price. The first thing we have to do is hire a detective—I know the perfect guy—and find out all we can about Sitting Bull. It's too bad he's not still a minor—we know he ran away from home. But you can't prosecute an adult for that. Still, he's bound to have a few skeletons in his closet. Miranda, what do you know about him?"

Suddenly I exist again! Their three bleary gazes fixed on her like spotlights. What *did* she know? He was a recovering alcoholic. He had a hair-trigger temper and a history of physical abuse. He'd had to survive on the streets by himself since he was seventeen, with almost no money. There might be a gold mine of things for a private detective to find. Miranda's mouth was full of peanut butter and crackers. She pretended she couldn't answer, giving herself time to think. Whose side was she on now? Just because she had suspicions about Adam, did she want to help sell him out? Did she really want to help her father get her grandmother's property, knowing what he wanted to do with it? "I don't know anything about him," she mumbled, which, after all, was the truth.

"Hey! You're only fifteen, aren't you?" Skip asked, looking at her with real interest. "Did he do anything funny to you, sweetheart? Because if he did, his ass is in jail tonight!"

"Cut it!" Richard slammed his beer can down, making Ariel jump. "Would you mind not making my daughter a pawn in your chess game, buddy?" He turned to Miranda. "He *didn't* do anything funny, did he?"

"No!"

"Good," Richard sighed.

"Not good!" Skip said. "That would have been our ticket. One night in the slammer and I bet he'd sign any document you put in front of him."

Richard's face was getting red. "You're talking about using my daughter like some kind of—"

"All right, Rich! Jeez!" Skip held up his hand. "It's all beside the point anyway. But this is my theory. You take a piece of trash like Adam, he's going to have something bad in his past, you just know it. I'll draw up a little contract for him to make a gift of this house and the acreage to you, and when we get some leverage over him—bam!"

"How many times have you done stuff like this before?" Ariel asked. She had emptied her wine bottle and reached down for a beer, apparently not caring what it tasted like at this point.

"Hey. I'm in business," Skip explained. "It's a game for winners, not whiners."

"I don't know," Richard said. "Maybe I just want to pack up and get out of here."

Skip pounded the coffee table with his fist. "This is your home, man! You can't let that little vermin run you off! Shit, I used to sit with you in that kitchen right there and watch Lila make cookies. Remember those vanilla things with the cherries?"

"Yeah." Richard lowered his eyes.

"Remember fishing in the canals? Remember riding our bikes all the way around the island? You were married in this house, Rich! Your whole life is here. Turtle Island belongs to people like you and me, Richard. You can't let that little twerp take everything from you just because Lila had one spiteful day in an attorney's office. Let's at least go down fighting, right?"

Richard picked up his beer. Fumbling, he adjusted his glasses. "It's blackmail, Skip. You're talking about blackmailing him."

"My first choice was to hire some boys to beat the crap out of him!" Skip said. "I'm trying to compromise here."

"It's just . . ." Richard gestured vaguely. "I don't think it's my style."

Skip took a fresh can from the pack and popped it aggressively. He swallowed four long gulps. "What is your style? Rolling over and playing dead? Letting this nobody come into your house and mess with your mother and your daughter and walk away with everything that's rightfully yours? And you're going to shake his hand like he beat you in a tennis game? What kind of a wimp are you?"

Richard was breathing hard. "You're just trying to push my buttons and make me—"

"Hey!" Skip held up both hands. "Why should I

care? Sooner or later, I'm gonna get my mall, whether I get the land from you or from him. Won't you feel like a fool then? If you run home to Ohio with your tail between your legs and Adam ends up cutting a deal with me, won't you feel stupid? That kid has the power to make a fool out of you and Lila and you're going to let him."

Richard ran his hands through his hair. He looked at Ariel, but she had slumped down and closed her eyes. Her breathing was deep and regular. "What exactly are you talking about doing?" Richard asked Skip.

"That's my boy! Just a little digging. A little treasure hunt. If we strike gold, we hold it over his head until he makes a deal with you. Hell, you can even make it reasonable, give him some money for good effort. You won't need any cash after you sell this property to me. So everybody would walk away with something. What's wrong with that?"

Richard suddenly turned to Miranda. "What do you think?"

She was stunned. "What do *I* think?"

"Yes. I'm a little confused, and I respect your opinion. Do you think there's anything wrong with looking into Adam's background?"

Looking? What could be wrong with looking? Then they would at least know if he was a cheap con artist or the good person Lila had believed him to be. It was information Miranda—and everyone—needed to know. "Do it," she said.

The next morning the telephone woke Miranda at eight o'clock.

"Hello?" she grumbled.

"Hi." It was Adam.

"What do you want?" Miranda sat up and tucked the sheet around her, as if the phone had eyes.

"I wanted to talk to you. Because of everything that . . . happened."

"What did you want me to say?" Miranda thought she sounded like a secretary.

There was a pause. "Well, you know! Did you see this coming? What am I going to do? Do you hate me now? Anything you have on your mind."

"No, I don't know and I'm not sure." Miranda held her breath. She wasn't used to being rough with people.

"Okay. Bye." *Click*. The dial tone roared like a giant bee.

"Damn." Miranda got out of bed. This was no way to start the day. Her body felt weak with sadness. *I could call him back*. She reached for the phone but stopped herself. Maybe they were enemies now. Except if he was this sleazy con artist, why call her now? He had what he wanted. Wouldn't it be his lawyer calling, telling them they had three days to pack up and go? He'd asked her what he should do. Maybe he was confused, looking for a friend. . . .

She walked out of the room so that the phone couldn't tempt her.

Their bedroom door was shut. Not a big surprise considering last night. When Miranda had gone to bed, they'd still been at it, out of beer and wine and passing around some old bottle of crème de menthe they found in the pantry closet. Miranda had left at the stage where they were finding everything hilarious and laughing too loud, like kids on a field trip. It wasn't pretty to watch.

Miranda decided to take advantage of their hangovers and go for a walk alone in the marsh. She needed to think, and she really didn't know how much more time they had. If Adam was angry, he might kick them out on the spot. Plus, it was what her grandmother had told her to do. *That's where you'll find me.*

But as she tiptoed down the hall, she heard the door creak behind her. Ariel peered out, looking as if she'd aged forty years and stuck her head in a blender. "Are you up?" she asked Miranda.

So it was true about the brain cells. "Yes," Miranda said. "You want me to make you some coffee?"

Ariel slumped against the door frame. "Oh, Jesus, yes." She emerged in a cloud of ice blue chiffon, held up by little silk straps. Usually Miranda thought her stepmother looked beautiful, but in this concoction she was like a horse in a ballet skirt. Or maybe Miranda was just down on the world.

In the kitchen, Ariel sat at the table and covered her face with her hands. Blond hair swept across her place mat.

"I'm never going to drink alcohol," Miranda said cheerfully, spooning coffee into her grandmother's percolator.

The phone rang. Ariel's body jerked like a live wire. *Adam?* "I'll get it!" Miranda hurried to the phone. "Hello?"

"Hello? Is this Mrs. Gates?"

"Mrs. Gates is dead," Miranda said, keeping an eye on Ariel, who looked as if she might slide off her chair.

"No, I mean Richard's wife. I don't remember your first name. This is Evelina Lincoln-Whitt."

Oh, Christ! "Her name is Ariel, but I'm not her. I'm Richard's daughter, Miranda."

"Oh. Well, are any of the adults there, dear?"

Miranda glanced at the "adult" in front of her and considered the one who was still unconscious. "No."

"Oh, well, I had hoped to come by this morning and make my selection. Usually on Fridays I go to the post office, and I like to be there at ten-thirty when they open. There's almost no line then. . . ."

Ariel lifted her head. "Who the hell is that?"

Miranda frowned at her.

"So I could be over either on my way to the post office, which would be between ten-thirty and ten-forty-five or on my way back, which would be between eleven-thirty and eleven-forty-five."

"Who the hell is ringing the phone all morning?" Richard yelled from the hall.

Miranda covered the mouthpiece. "Quiet!" she shouted. Then she spoke into the phone. "Ms. Whitt?"

"Lincoln-Whitt, dear."

"Great. Whatever. Make it ten-thirty. Okay?"

"Well, it would be sometime between ten-thirty and ten-forty-five. . . . "

"Yeah, great. I've gotta run."

"So we're agreed that it would be between—"

"Ten-thirty and ten-forty-five! Good-bye!"

"Good-bye!"

Miranda sighed. This would turn into another one of those stories about how rude young people were.

Richard staggered into the kitchen. "It's like it's been going off like a fire alarm every ten minutes! Oh, thank god, coffee!" He turned to Ariel. "Hi," he said in a funny tone.

"Hi." She sounded funny, too.

Miranda turned around quickly, but they'd already heard themselves and put neutral expressions on their faces.

Miranda poured them each a cup of black coffee. "The first one," she said, "was a wrong number, and the second one was Evelina Lincoln-Whitt. She wants to come pick out her loot. Between ten-thirty and ten-forty-five."

"What's her problem?" Richard demanded. "Does she think she has to hurry before I hock all the stuff?"

"It's not yours to hock," Ariel said.

Richard gave her a look that was almost hateful. Ariel accepted the look calmly. Then she said to Miranda, "Call her back and tell her no. Your dad and I need to talk today."

"We needed to talk last night," he said.

Miranda wanted to leave. "I think I'm going for a walk."

"Where?" Richard said, in a tone that made it clear he was afraid she was visiting Adam.

"Out in the marsh. I want to enjoy it while we have it."

"That's good," Ariel said. "Because we need—"

"*You* need!" Richard corrected. "*You're* the one who has all the issues all of a sudden. And what considerate timing, as I'm grieving over my mother and losing everything I have!"

Miranda knew if she didn't get out of there, she'd be pulling jury service. Still, she wanted to stay and see if this was serious. "You guys, if you had a fight last night when you were both drinking . . ."

"No, it's not that," Ariel said. "It's just that when I drink it makes me more honest."

"Well, this whole week, you've been so honest I thought you needed a clinic!" Richard shot back.

"Your mother's death has upset me!"

Richard's eyebrows shot up. "Upset *you*!"

"Okay, we're both upset. We're all upset." Ariel's eyes looked teary.

"Which is why"—Richard switched to his professional voice—"this is not the time to talk about any kind of major issues. I'm going to take a hot shower and get centered. We should both do that before we launch into—"

"You can shave and shower and put on a cashmere sweater, but the problem is still going to be there!" Ariel said.

Richard gave her that look again. He finished his coffee in two gulps and stood up. "The one thing you have never had, Ari, is timing. Anybody looking at this from the outside would say maybe you have doubts about our relationship all of a sudden because you found out I'm not going to inherit all the money you may have been counting on. Naturally, I don't believe that . . . but you see how it looks. Or how it makes you look." He walked out with his head down. In a second they heard the shower start up.

Ariel stared at the doorway he'd gone through, her eyes the same stony blue as her nightgown. "You can't win an argument with a shrink," she said almost to herself. "Because they always say something to make you hate yourself."

"Ariel," Miranda said softly. "What's going on?"

Ariel's eyes shifted and turned vulnerable as a baby's. She almost said something, then jumped up from the table and ran off. A second shower started. Now they would fight it out in the hot-water arena.

The phone rang. Miranda jumped, tried to ignore it. It kept going, jangling and vibrating like something trying to explode. She almost felt the ringing in her blood. She backed away from it and hit the back door with both hands. It flew open and struck the outside wall.

She could still hear the phone as she ran through the yard, watching her sneakers pound the wet grass, scattering dewdrops. She ran with all her strength toward the marsh, where the birds were singing loudly enough to drown out anything.

CHAPTER

twelve

The minute she was alone, walking the marsh trails, Miranda felt a wave of grief for her grandmother. It was a body feeling, spreading up from the pit of her stomach, kicking her diaphragm, compressing her lungs, squeezing her throat. Her hands trembled. Her eyes watered. Only her legs seemed impervious, pacing along, pulling her deeper into the wetlands, deeper than she'd ever gone before.

She realized she was angry, too. She hated what was going on back at the house, all the wrangling and maneuvering—everyone taking sides and fighting for positions. Lila was lost in this. No one ever talked about her or mentioned her name.

Miranda slowed her steps a little, scanning to make

sure she wasn't lost. The path had twisted and turned. Her orientation was off. In the distance, in a direction she didn't expect, she made out the line of tall cypress trees at the back of the house. They looked very far away. Maybe it would be a good thing to get lost. Everyone would pull together, searching for her. They would realize what was really important in life. *Great idea for a TV movie, but it never happens in real life.* In real life, people died before you even got to know them. In real life you could fall in love with someone and then wonder if he was bad after all. Or your stepmother could walk out on your father. Or your father could destroy everything your grandmother had stood for. Or your mother could die . . .

This thought startled Miranda so badly she stopped walking, just stopped dead in her tracks, listening to the blood pound in her temples, drowning out the hum of the cicadas. She never thought about her mother. There was nothing to think about. Her mother was . . . just a story she'd heard other adults tell. There were no memories, so there was nothing to feel sad about.

Maybe that's why you have no memories.

It was almost like an alien voice in her head. Miranda began to walk again, but this time it was a slow, cautious, almost a stalking gait. Was she deliberately squashing memories of her mother to avoid the feelings that went with them?

Ever since she'd come to Florida, she'd felt like a different person. Back in Ohio she was calm, poised, on top of things. She sat back and watched other people have lives. She remembered a party she'd attended with her father when she was twelve. A woman had said to her, "It must be terrible having a psychiatrist for a father—does he analyze you all the time?" Before Miranda could give an answer, her father had said, "Miranda's so stable there's nothing to analyze."

She'd been so proud of the compliment at the time, but . . . wasn't he also saying there was nothing to her? As if she didn't have an identity at all? "You were the best baby," he often told her. "You never cried." How could that be? In the whole history of the world, how could there be a baby who never cried? Shouldn't he, as a psychiatrist, see that as a problem in a baby?

Miranda stopped and looked for the cypress trees again. They were really tiny now, but she could still see them.

That's where you'll find me. It was true. Lila was here. She was Florida—warm and colorful and chaotic. Noisy. Emotional. So different from her son. So different from Miranda, except . . . since Miranda had come here, some new part of her had been waking up. Maybe it was the Lila part of her. Or maybe the part that was like her mother . . .

A memory grazed her consciousness—a snapshot of a

178

perfect little blue china cup, the bluest blue in the world, with warm, reddish gold liquid pouring into it. Fragrant steam, gingery, like Lila, jasmine, like her mother's name. If she looked up from the little teacup, she would see her mother's face. She would look into her mother's eyes and see what color they were. But the memory popped like a soap bubble and left her alone, surrounded by waves of tall grass, rippling in streams of wind. "Oh, Mommy," she said in a little girl's voice. Finally the grief went down to her legs. Her knees buckled. She knelt on the trail, head down, hoping for and fearing tears. "Oh, Mommy," she said again, but it was forced this time. The spirit had left her.

As she trudged back toward the house, she saw someone lying facedown in the grass beside the main house. Adam. Miranda broke into a trot, panicking, imagining Skip Wilson going too far and pulling out a handgun. . . .

But then Adam's body sort of wiggled in the grass, as if he was adjusting his position. A few more yards and she could see he was reaching his arm into the crawl space under the porch and talking to himself. *He's flipped. It was too much for him. He's planting a bomb.*

Pride and curiosity waged a quick war in her brain. Curiosity won. She swerved in his direction. Indian or

not, he obviously didn't hear her. He was totally involved in something under the porch, straining his arm
to reach it, muttering, "Come on, come on."

Miranda stood right over him for several seconds, trying not to stare at the seat of his jeans. "What's up?" she
finally said.

His whole body jerked, curving and drawing the
knees up, one hand flying to protect his face. *Battered
child,* Miranda reminded herself. "I'm sorry," she said.
"What are you doing down there?"

Red-faced, he brushed grass off himself to calm
down. "It's Wesa, he's under there and he won't come
out. I don't know how long he's been there, maybe since
Lila collapsed. He's acting all feral and crazy."

"Oh." Miranda put her hand up to her mouth. The
guilt almost nauseated her. "I never even thought about
him this whole week!"

"Yeah." Adam sat on his heels. "We're really carrying
on Lila's values, aren't we? Nobody even remembered
to take care of her goddamned cat."

Miranda got down on all fours and peered through
the latticework. The sandy dirt was carpeted with pine
needles and paper trash, in various states of decay. Wesa
was wedged into a corner, trembling. Some substance,
like grease or tar, streaked his fur. His eyes looked wild.
Scary.

"If I go to that other side, where he is, he just comes

over here," Adam said. "But maybe if you go over there, he'll come close enough for me to get him."

Miranda tried to remember that Adam was a potential enemy and that she shouldn't be cooperating with him. It seemed like a really stupid thought now. "He'll just go to the middle. Maybe we could squirt the hose in there . . ."

"That's cruel!" Adam said.

"It's crueler to leave him there! He might starve. He's obviously too upset to take care of himself."

Adam looked unconvinced. "Cats are stubborn, Miranda. He could just sit there getting soaked and then we'd feel bad because we'd have made him more uncomfortable."

"Yeah."

"I've tried calling, but maybe if you did it . . ."

"Me?" Miranda said. "He knows you a lot better than me."

"I know, but you have a female voice and it's . . . you have such a soft, pretty voice."

Miranda had been squinting under the porch, but his tone made her look up, and she was caught in a brown-eyed gaze that made her want to kiss him. "I do?"

"Yeah." He looked away. "Didn't anybody ever tell you that?"

Miranda wondered what was wrong with her for ever doubting him. Here was a guy who had just inherited a fortune, and he was crawling around in the dirt, trying to help a cat. What more did she need to know? "Adam. After we get him out, we need to talk. About everything that's . . . happening."

"Sure, okay." He ducked his head as if he was afraid of what kind of talk it would be.

Miranda flattened herself in the grass and peered through the lattice. Wesa tried to step back, squashing himself into the corner. His tail whipped around like a live wire.

"Wesa? Sweetheart? It's me, Miranda. Adam and I want you to come out, baby."

Wesa's mouth opened to emit a strange, low moan. It didn't sound friendly.

"Aren't you hungry?" Miranda asked. "We want to feed you." She turned to Adam. "Go in the house and get his cat food. Maybe we can lure him."

"Hello? You want me to go in there with your father? I'll go to my house and get some baloney or something."

"Okay, okay. Just do it."

Adam took off and returned with a bag of turkey slices.

"Oh, boy," said Miranda to the cat. "Look, sweetie. Turkey. Mmmmm . . ." She took out a slice and dangled it through the slats with her fingers.

Wesa pumped his nose like a rabbit.

"It's working!" Miranda said. "Come on, baby, you can have the whole package if you come out."

Wesa's body flowed a few inches forward, like a viscous liquid.

"You're a genius, Miranda!" Adam said, watching over her shoulder. Miranda tried not to notice how good he smelled, like soap and cypress trees.

Wesa seemed to unroll like a long carpet, moving with his torso low to the ground, every muscle alert as he inched forward.

A thundering noise above them froze the cat in his tracks.

Miranda looked up. Evelina Lincoln-Whitt was lumbering down the porch steps with a bentwood rocker over her head. "Oh, shoot, you scared the cat!" Miranda told her.

Ms. Lincoln-Whitt paused, blinked at Miranda and Adam and hurried on. She loaded the rocker into her Ford Explorer and took off in a spray of gravel.

Miranda and Adam glanced at each other, then lay down to look at Wesa again. He had retreated to his corner and looked more nervous than ever. Miranda coaxed him and brandished the meat, but got no response. "I think he thinks we lured him into a trap and now he doesn't trust us!"

"Dammit," Adam said. "We may have to squirt water on him after all."

"But he's hysterical. What we need is something to calm him down, not rile him up. I've got a really stupid idea."

"Well," Adam said, "we don't have any intelligent ones."

"Let's sing to him."

Adam laughed. "Yeah. Good. What movie is this from?"

"No, no. We could sing 'Over the Rainbow.' It's Lila's favorite. She sang it all the time, didn't she?"

"She sure did."

"So Wesa knows it. It might be comforting. What do you think?"

"I think it's nicer than the hose idea. Let's try it."

Side by side, lying in the grass, propped up on their elbows, they began to sing a giggly, broken chorus of the song. Wesa looked at them in surprise. After a second they grew more serious and their voices began to blend sweetly. Adam's was very deep, and Miranda's was more alto than soprano. They struck an odd harmony, like clarinet and oboe. Members of the same family. It was so striking, they glanced at each other in surprise, not wanting to interrupt the song, but clearly acknowledging that something special was unfolding.

Wesa's eyes responded first. The wild look flickered and faded. The eyelids drooped repeatedly—a cat's version of a smile. The rigid body began to loosen and settle against the wood. Finally Wesa sat down and tucked his paws under, not coming forward, but definitely at ease.

" 'Where troubles melt like lemon drops away above the chimney tops, that's where you'll find me . . .' "

A wave of emotion about Lila choked Miranda, but she kept going as Adam slowly stood up and walked around the porch to the other side. Wesa turned his head as Adam approached, but didn't move. Adam sat down in the grass and reached through the lattice, stroking Wesa's fur as they finished the song.

He lifted the cat carefully, pulling him through the wooden slats and into his arms.

"We did it!" he called to Miranda.

She ran to him with the bag of turkey. "Here, let's feed you, sweetheart. You must be starved! Wesa, we're so sorry we forgot you!"

Adam set the cat down. "Don't give him more than a few slices at first. If he's starving, he'll eat too fast and make himself sick."

Wesa seemed to inhale the turkey. Adam went off and returned with a cereal bowl full of water. They gave Wesa two more slices of meat and then set him in front of the bowl. His pink tongue sliced in and out of the water, making ripples on the surface.

Miranda touched her heart. "What a relief!" She looked at Adam and saw the serious look in his eyes.

"So let's talk," he said.

Miranda felt ashamed. "Adam, we don't need to talk. I've just been . . . really stupid. Maybe I just felt confused because of Lila dying, or maybe I'm trying to be loyal to my father even though I really don't think . . ."

"Say it."

Miranda hung her head. "I think he's wrong about a lot of things."

Adam touched her arm. "That doesn't mean you don't love him. Which is more than I could say for my father."

She looked up. "I know. I guess for a while there I was trying to be loyal to everyone."

"Sometimes you have to choose a side."

"They're going to hire a private detective to investigate you. Skip Wilson thinks he can find something to hold over you and make you sell the land."

"What?"

"But there's nothing they could find, is there?"

Adam ran his hand back and forth across his mouth. "Oh, god."

Miranda's heart quickened. "What?"

"I jumped bail in Tennessee. My old man got me busted for assault, and then he bailed me out like it was a big favor, and that's when I took off. I know now it was stupid . . ."

"How could you have been arrested? I thought he was the one who beat you up!"

"Well, yeah, but I never called the cops on him for the seventeen years he did it. The one night I hit back, he dialled 911 like a shot. If I'd stayed and had a hearing and told my story, it might have been okay, but if you jump bail . . . it's a pretty bad thing."

Miranda suddenly realized they were sitting right by the house. "Yes, Adam!" she whispered. "It is!"

"They could find that out," Adam said. He glanced around as if choosing a direction to run in. "They could get me busted again! Miranda, you just don't know how bad that is, getting handcuffed and locked up. I'd kill myself if I thought that was going to happen again. Why the hell did Lila do this to me?"

"Shhh. Calm down. They don't want you arrested. They want you to sign the land over to them."

His eyes were getting as wild as the cat's had been. "But I can't do that, either. Lila trusted me to take care of all this for her. Miranda, what am I going to do? I can't just sit here like a rabbit in a trap and wait for them to get me!"

Miranda had never seen Adam, or anyone, for that matter, look so scared. "What happened to you in jail?" she whispered.

"Nothing!" he said, making it clear he understood her question perfectly. "It isn't that anything has to happen in jail. . . . It's just . . . If it hasn't happened to you, you can't know. You're in a cage. It's up to someone else if you ever get out. You're helpless. You—"

"Okay, stop! You're making yourself—"

"You just don't *know*!"

"Okay!" Miranda forced herself to breathe calmly. "I'll talk to Daddy. I don't think his heart is really in any of this, and I think he might listen to me. If I tell him honestly what you told me—"

"No, no, please don't do that!"

"Okay, then, if I just reason with him. He knows I . . . care about you, and I don't think he would do anything to hurt me. And really, deep down, he knows he and Skip are wrong."

"I don't get that feeling." Adam hugged himself.

"Believe me, I know. I feel bad, Adam, because I haven't been sticking up for you. Maybe things wouldn't have gone this far if I had. But I'll go in right now and talk to him. He doesn't want to blackmail you. He's just upset because Lila, you know, sort of picked you to be her son and not him."

"I know."

"He's really a good man, Adam."

"He hates me. And he listens to that friend of his."

"He listens to me, too. I'll go in there right now."

Adam grabbed her hand. "Thank you."

Miranda wanted to say more, but some kind of embarrassment choked her. "Lindsay Baker said a whole bunch of stuff about you to me. Like that you were a big liar and I shouldn't trust you."

His eyes flicked back and forth, studying Miranda. "She's jealous of you. She and I never clicked. Or she clicked and I didn't, which is worse. You know all this. Why would you even listen to her?"

"I'm not accusing you, I'm confessing that I did listen. I'm sorry."

"It's okay. There's been a lot of . . . just stuff. We're all mixed up."

Miranda squeezed his hand. "Yeah."

He bit his lip. "Not just the stuff with Lila."

"Right."

"I mean . . ." Adam blushed. "We're . . . when you start to fall in love, you get, or at least I get . . . you know, paranoid. . . ."

"Yeah."

"Because you care and it scares you."

"Yeah."

"And you start babbling like a moron while the other person just keeps saying 'yeah.' " He laughed.

Miranda laughed. "Yeah."

He pulled her to him. It was a hungry kiss, as if his mouth were searching for something. His body felt tight and scared in her arms. Miranda almost wanted to push away. She knew now how much he needed her. She

189

knew they had both just crossed the border into a place they would never leave.

"Okay," she whispered, pulling back.

"I'm sorry. I'm still thinking about . . . what could happen."

"I know. It's okay. I just don't want Daddy to come out of the house and find . . ."

"Right." Blushing, he turned to look at Wesa, who had curled up for a nap on the pine needles.

"I'll go talk to him." Miranda stood up, shakily.

Adam didn't meet her eyes. "Okay."

"Are we . . . still going to have our ceremony tonight?"

He looked up, smiled a little. "Still want to?"

"Yes, of course. Meet me out on the main trail at midnight."

"Miranda, maybe not. Maybe you shouldn't sneak out."

"No. I need to do it. Don't back out on me."

"I won't. Good . . . Good luck."

"I won't need it, Adam. I can convince him." *I have to, now.*

Adam stroked the cat a few times, then got up. "Okay, see you tonight." He walked away with his head down.

Miranda began to rehearse her speech as she climbed

the steps. *Daddy, I think you really need to look at everything that's happened and figure out where you stand.*

She opened the front door and went inside.

Her father was sitting on the couch, elbows on knees, a tent of fingers covering his nose and mouth. He was staring at the carpet, staring into his own thoughts. It was the third set of terrified eyes Miranda had seen that morning. Her speech crumbled.

"What is it?" she said.

"Go say good-bye to your stepmother," he said, and then his voice climbed three octaves. "She's packing."

CHAPTER

thirteen

Ariel's blue suitcase was open on the bed, a pile of
pastel nightgowns and underwear jumbled in the
bottom. She was on her hands and knees in the closet.

"Have you gone nuts?" Miranda asked.

Ariel stood up, swinging her hair back. Her face was
red, and her arms were full of high heels. "Don't try to
talk me out of it," she said. "I made up my mind, and I
know what I have to do. You can either make it easier
for me or harder."

Miranda sat on the bed. "Let me think about that."
She jumped back as a hail of pumps cascaded into the
suitcase. "You're supposed to pack your shoes first." Miranda began unloading.

"Hey!"

"I'm going to organize it for you."

They stared at each other for a second. Enemies. Friends. Family.

"You're leaving me, too," Miranda said. "Do I get an explanation?"

Ariel sat on the bed, watching Miranda neatly replace her shoes in rows. "It's pretty simple. I don't really love Richard."

"He's not acting like himself right now."

"I know. But even when he is . . ."

"This is a bad time, Ari. He's losing everything at once."

"Don't do that to me."

"But it's true. He lost his mother, his house . . ."

"If I stay here because he needs me and help him through it, then that's the wrong message! See, I know I've done a bad thing and I want to undo it. The quicker—"

"What do you mean, a bad thing?"

"I married him! I thought I was in love when I wasn't! I let you think I was going to be your step-mother . . ."

Miranda realized she was biting her nails. "What's so terrible about Daddy?"

"Nothing! He's a nice man. I've just been realiz-ing—"

193

"How come you realized it the minute he lost his money?" That had sort of slipped out, but Miranda didn't want to take it back, either.

Ariel exhaled slowly, a soundless whistle. "You can think that if you want to, but it's not true."

"Well, the timing is pretty amazing."

"Not true. Think about it. This is the first really bad thing I've seen Richard go through. I should be feeling all loving and supportive. My heart should be going out to him, but . . . I just feel like I want to get away from all this."

"Maybe you're just a bitch," Miranda said in a low voice.

Ariel stared at her. "I'm not, Miranda, what I am is honest with myself. People get married for all kinds of reasons. I don't know what I was looking for in your father . . . but it wasn't what I really needed."

Miranda stood up. "He's had a hard time! Why are you judging him—"

"I'm not, honey." Ariel's hand trailed after Miranda into empty space. "I'm just *seeing* Richard now. Or maybe it's myself I'm seeing clearly. I just know what I have to do."

Miranda gently kicked the bed. "I guess you've made up your mind."

"I don't lie to myself, Miranda. Sometimes I wish I did. Will you try to understand?"

Miranda began folding underwear. "I don't have to like it."

Ariel got up slowly and went to the dresser. She returned with a pile of sweats and jeans. She seemed to be ignoring all the expensive dresses in her closet. Maybe she was leaving behind everything Richard had paid for. "That's another thing." Ariel gave Miranda a lopsided smile. "The best part of the whole marriage was being friends with you."

Miranda's breath caught. "I need a hug, Ari."

Ariel put the clothes on the bed and held out her arms. Miranda closed her eyes, breathing in Ariel's clean, ferny scent. For the last time.

"Where are you going?" Miranda asked.

"Malibu, I guess. My brother has a house there. He's always good at times like these, since he has his life totally together." Ariel was in the bathroom now, dumping things into her cosmetic bag.

"Hooray for him."

"I'm going to file right away. I don't want a thing. It'll be quick. You might think it's cruel, but it's kind that way. It's like pulling off a Band-Aid. You gotta do it fast." Ariel came out of the bathroom and looked around. She added a stuffed rabbit and some kind of blank book to her suitcase and closed it. Miranda noticed her wedding ring was already off. She looked young, maybe because she wore no makeup.

Miranda leaned back against the headboard. "I'm glad someone likes for things to happen fast. Everything happens way too fast for me."

A car horn sounded outside. "There's my taxi!" There was a slight note of panic in Ariel's voice.

"Ariel?" Richard called from the living room. His tone of voice was as normal as when he called her to tell her the pizza was being delivered.

"Oh, god!" Ariel said. "Good-bye, Miranda. I love you." She kissed Miranda on her forehead—another waft of fern, a final brush of silky hair—then hefted her bags. "If Richard tries to help the cabdriver with these bags, so help me I'll kill him," she muttered.

Miranda didn't follow her. She sat on the bed, feeling like a drained battery. "I love you, too," she said to the emptiness. Slowly she eased herself up and crossed the hall to Lila's room to look out the front window. Her father was indeed carrying Ariel's bags. He loaded the trunk of the cab and stood talking to Ariel while the cabdriver stood by, looking impatient. Miranda was sure her father was giving Ariel all kinds of advice on airline tickets and connections. Ariel cut him off by saying something while placing a hand on his shoulder. He stopped speaking, and his whole body slumped. Ariel kissed his forehead exactly the way she had kissed Miranda, and got into the cab. The driver, Ariel's age, gave her an admiring look as she got in. Then he closed the door in a proprietary way, slid into the driver's seat and started the engine. Miranda and her father both watched the taxi drive out of sight. Then Miranda sat down on Lila's bed. The front door slammed. The door of Richard's room slammed. Then there was no sound at all.

Naturally, there was a long phone call to Skip Wilson that afternoon. And naturally he came over with a twelve-pack that evening. Miranda stayed in her room, able to pick up only the loudest bursts of laughter and the heavily accented words, like *bitch*. Skip was doing most of the talking. Richard was either silently agreeing or too drunk to answer.

Miranda wondered if they had been like this the whole time they were growing up—her father perpetually hurt and misunderstood, Skip making it better with alcohol and insults to the "enemy." Miranda was thinking about the things Ariel had said. How was it that this brilliant psychiatrist seemed to need so much help to cope with his problems? Could you practice one thing and preach another? Or did coming back to the place where he'd been a kid make him childish again? Miranda pictured her father as a teenager and realized to her surprise that he'd have been a nerd, a blushing, stammering guy whose glasses slid down his nose. If she'd met him in school, she probably wouldn't have been friends with him! It was a thought too spooky to pursue.

By eleven-thirty the beer and Skip were gone and Richard was asleep on the couch, surrounded by empties. He was sweating in his sleep and breathing hard, as if his dreams were strenuous. Miranda cleaned up the mess, mostly to see how deeply he was sleeping. He never moved a muscle. It was the perfect situation for sneaking out of the house.

Feeling a strange excitement, Miranda went to Lila's room, looking for props. She had hoped to have more time to plan this "ceremony," but too many other things had happened. All she had was her original idea, that she wanted to paint her face with Lila's lipstick to make herself visible to the spirits. She realized, with a sudden jolt, that her mother was in that world, too.

She sat at Lila's vanity table, rummaging through the huge collection of lipsticks. Lila had certainly loved the Avon Lady. Miranda opened several tubes, looking for a good war paint color. She settled on Chili Pepper. She put the tube in her pocket, deciding instinctively that the painting itself was part of the ceremony and should happen in the marsh.

With the same kind of instinct, she opened Lila's jewelry box and took out several strings of iridescent beads, looping them around her neck, wrists and ankles. This was the right path, decorating herself with Lila's things. She opened another box and found a pile of silk scarves in delicate colors. She tied one around her hair, one around her waist and one around each arm. When she stood and twirled for the mirror, the beads rattled softly and the scarves flew out like wings and haloes. Miranda saw how much she was smiling, and it made her smile even more. She knew Lila would approve. As a final touch, she sprayed a mist of Lila's Hawaiian White Ginger cologne all over herself. Her eyes and nose burned with the scent and the memories it carried. She studied her reflection and thought that somehow, her whole appearance had changed since she came to Florida. Her hair, carefully trimmed at home, had grown curlier and wilder; her eyes had a deeper, sadder shine. For the first time in her life, Miranda saw a resemblance to the photographs of her mother. "My wild side," she said softly. As she turned and walked from the mirror, Lila's beads and scarves clinked and whispered in agreement.

Adam did not adorn himself. He met Miranda in the backyard dressed in jeans and a white T-shirt. However, he did have the wooden box from his dresser.

"What's that?" Miranda asked.

"Medicine bundle," he said. "Magic stuff. You'll see. And look at you! You look like a belly dancer! Are you going to do the Dance of the Seven Veils?"

Miranda smiled. "You never know." She felt beautiful as they walked along, the scarves swirling and wafting in the breeze.

He took her hand. "Will you marry me when you grow up?"

Miranda stopped walking and pulled her hand back. "Cut it out," she said.

"No." He faced her on the path, looking straight into her eyes. "I mean it. You're part of Lila and this place. You're part of everything I love. I won't ever find anyone like you again. No matter how much your father hates me, will you come back? Next summer maybe, or whenever you can? Will you promise not to forget me?"

Miranda was stunned. She tried to laugh. "Adam, you're just reacting to Lila's cologne that I'm wearing or something. . . ."

He started walking again, head down. "I'm sorry."

Miranda hurried to catch up with him. Her bracelets and necklaces rattled harshly. "I feel like that, too, Adam. I just don't want to think about that right now, okay?"

"Okay." His head stayed down.

"Adam." She pulled his arm to make him stop.

They faced each other on the path. Miranda reached

up, put her arms around his neck. The scarf in her hair brushed his cheek. He closed his eyes. Miranda pulled his face down, kissed, kissed again, parted her lips and kissed, leaned against his body and kissed. Her necklaces pressed painfully into her chest. Adam ground against her, put his tongue in her mouth. His hands began to stroke and fondle. They both pulled back at once.

"Sorry, sorry," he said.

"I'll come back," Miranda said, ducking to look into his lowered eyes. "I'll always come back to you."

They walked deep into the marsh, past all the landmarks Miranda knew, but Adam seemed to have his bearings. "We should look for a place that feels sacred," he said.

Miranda decided that what he called sacred, she called spooky. Everything around them seemed weird tonight. Cypress fronds fluttered in the wind like old shawls on gnarled bodies. Red and gold eyes glowed in the thickets beside streams. Alligators honked bass warnings. Tree frogs seemed to scream. The path was difficult to see. There was a half-moon.

"Eeek!" Miranda stopped and pointed. Ahead in the path was a tiny, upright figure, about eight inches tall, walking toward them on two legs.

Adam laughed. "It's an owl, a burrowing owl. They're nesting now. She's probably got a burrow close to the path and she thinks we're a threat. Relax," he said to the little dark shape. "We're just passing through."

The owl took wing and sheared the air beside them, landing in the path behind.

"She's just trying to scare us," Adam said.

"It works!" Miranda looked over her shoulder at the tiny glaring figure.

"I called Lila's lawyer this afternoon," Adam said abruptly.

"You did?"

He hugged himself. "Yeah. I thought I should. Not that it would help me if your father digs up a bunch of bad stuff on me, but I thought I should talk to some-one."

"Did you tell him about your . . . past?"

"No. I'll cross that bridge when I get to it. We had other things to argue about. He says I should get you guys off the property as fast as I can, like you should have been gone yesterday, but I said you came for the summer and you should have the summer. I'm not real anxious to rattle around in that big house anyway."

"But you should kick us out!" Miranda said. "The longer Daddy stays in Florida, the more time he has to hatch plots!"

"I know, but I feel sorry for him, too. He grew up in

Lila's house. Part of me believes the property is more his than mine, no matter what some legal papers say. If he wasn't bent on destroying everything, I'd give him the deed myself."

"You're crazy!"

Adam stuffed his hands in his pockets. "That's pretty much what the lawyer told me. And I had to pay him to say that!"

"Skip was over tonight, but they didn't talk about you. There's a new enemy. Ariel left."

"What?"

Miranda's voice shook slightly. "She's gone. Took off."

"With everything else that's going on?"

"That's what I said."

"So, your dad's lost his inheritance, mother and wife. In case anyone's keeping score."

"He is," Miranda said. "Why don't you look at my score while you're at it? Mother, grandmother, step-mother."

Adam took her hand.

It was long after midnight, Miranda was sure. "How big is this marsh?"

"There." Adam pointed. "That's the kind of place I was looking for."

Ahead of them the ground rose slightly, making a little round hilltop. Surrounding it were four tall slash pines. "It's like a little stage," Miranda said.

"This is where Lila wants us to stop. She'll come here if we call her."

Miranda shuddered. Adam said this in a completely serious tone. Miranda was partly playing, but she realized Adam believed in what they were doing. He climbed the hill and walked around on it, as if testing the feel of the turf under his feet. "Come on up," he commanded.

Clinking and billowing, Miranda followed him. They stood side by side on the high ground. "Feel it, feel the place. The power is coming right up out of the ground."

Miranda wasn't sure she felt that. But just being elevated a few feet gave her a skewed and weird panorama of the marsh. Now she could look down and see the lacy network of silver-black streams around them, the stirrings of wind and animals in the foliage. Miranda felt she was looking back to a time when the whole world was like this, a silent black swamp churning out life and death cycles like a sluggish old machine.

Adam knelt on the ground. He took a key from around his neck and opened the box, removing a compass and a small cloth bag.

"What's that?" Miranda pointed to the bag.

"Cracked corn. I want to make an offering to the four

directions. And the birds can enjoy it in the morning. I thought Lila would like that."

Adam peered at his compass, locating the cardinal points. Then he reached in his pack and extracted a white quartzlike stone, a heavy dark stone, a chunk of turquoise and a conch shell, using them to mark the directions. They corresponded eerily with the placement of the pine trees. Then he stood up, so straight-backed he almost looked unnatural, and, reciting something under his breath, threw a handful of corn in each of the directions. When he was done, he spoke in a loud, clear voice. "Thank you for guiding us to this hilltop and for your protection while we are here."

Miranda felt so nervous, she wanted to make a joke, but instead she just watched as he took a little bundle of dried herbs out and lit it with a match. "Sage," he said as a heavy, sweet smoke surrounded them. "To purify the hill and us." He swirled the heavy smoke around in a circle, then passed the sage branch over his own body and around Miranda's. He blew it out and stamped it carefully underfoot.

Miranda suddenly felt like jumping in. "Now," she said, "we will paint our faces, so the spirits can see us." She took the lipstick out of her pocket and uncapped it. "I'll do you and you do me."

Adam laughed softly. "Just don't make me look ridiculous."

Guided by impulse, Miranda drew two parallel lines, like an equal sign, on Adam's left cheek. She hesitated and then drew a red sun with rays on the other side of his face. Then she handed him the tube. She held perfectly still as he painted her lips, then drew something at the corner of her left eye.

"What is it?" Miranda asked.

"Three teardrops," he said. "For your lost mothers."

"Oh!" Miranda put her hand over her heart and struggled with a sudden urge to cry.

"Now we'll do one more thing," Adam said. He reached into the pack and took out a shiny black object. It was a little carved figure, an exquisite, tiny statue of a raven. "This is a Zuni fetish," he whispered to Miranda. "They're all made by hand, very expensive to buy. Lila sent for this for my birthday last year. Because she and I both have an affinity for the grackles. So he's my power animal, my guide to other worlds. Everyone has a helper like this who can come forward if asked. Some people have more than one."

Miranda thought of her vision the night Lila died. "The grackle is my animal, too. One of them has been . . . coming forward ever since I came here."

"Then this little fetish will fly for both of us," Adam said. He cupped the bird in his hands as if it were alive and made a tossing gesture, as one would do to help a fledgling. "Black Bird, please travel to the spirit world, where Miranda and I can't go. Call our grandmother Lila back to us, just for a minute. We're her children and we love her. We want to say good-bye and ask her to comfort us. Then we will set her free."

Miranda stared at the serious, almost beautiful expression in his eyes. Had he read all this somewhere or was he making it up as he went along? Whatever it was, Miranda found it more moving than the real funeral had been. Adam set the bird on the ground. A sudden gust of wind struck Miranda's face, and the scarf pulled free from her hair and soared on an updraft, floating away into the darkness. She watched it, and suddenly she felt as if she were the scarf, floating high above the network of silver-black watercourses, skimming the tops of trees and falling, plunging down to the earth, into the water, into blackness.

Then there was a window, a dark window in which Miranda saw the ghost of her own reflection. "Grandma?" she called, and immediately Lila's face appeared. Lila smiled and held her hand out to Miranda. But just as quickly as she had come, she was gone. The window was gone.

Miranda found herself in her old playroom, in the old house they had before they bought the condo. She was small, in a chair that was too big for her. There were strawberries on the curtains. She saw the teacup again, bright and blue like a morning glory. The warm, fire-color tea splashing in.

"Shall we give some tea to your bear, too?"

A pink feather boa shedding its fluff freely into the air as Mommy poured the tea—jasmine-like-my-name—and tipped the little cow creamer and dug a pretty spoon into the strawberry sugar bowl. Miranda liked it sweet. "Cambric tea," Mommy said, "means with sugar and milk."

Ginger and jasmine, clouds of hot flower steam, and the little girl lifted her eyes this time to the freckled arms inside the pink feather boa, up past the pointed chin and happy smile, up to the Gypsy curls and the silly, floppy hat. Mommy.

"Hey!" Adam had grabbed Miranda's arm.

Somehow she was standing, leaning forward as if straining to leap into her vision. "Green!" she cried. "My mother's eyes were green!"

CHAPTER

fourteen

They walked back in silence. Miranda wondered if Adam had the same strange feeling she had—like waking from a deep sleep and not being able to think right away. Or, no, it was like the feeling when you came out of the swimming pool and all your skin felt new. No, that wasn't it, either. It was like trying to walk after jumping on a trampoline, only with the brain, not the legs.

Miranda felt porous, absorbent. The trills and cries from the swamp, the warm wet air, the blackness of the sky, were all soaking into her, spreading through her fibers like permanent dye.

Adam had said, as he pulled Miranda back from the brink, "Did you see a vision?"

Miranda had been crying. "Yes. You?"

He had lowered his eyes. "Yes."

That was all. They hadn't exchanged stories. Maybe Adam thought it would break a sacred rule to tell about them.

Miranda didn't want to talk anyway. She didn't want to disturb the peacefulness in her mind. She did take Adam's hand, though. It was warm and solid as a sun-heated stone. She knew she would remember this night forever.

As they came to the edge of the marsh, Miranda realized the sky had lightened. The trees had lost their ghostly paleness and were now black silhouettes.

"Uh-oh." Adam's hand tightened on Miranda's.

She looked ahead. There was another silhouette, in the open kitchen door. Her father, his arms folded, leaning against the frame. Miranda couldn't tell if he'd already seen them or not, but in any case, he soon would.

She dropped Adam's hand. Adam pulled one of the scarves from her arm and began scrubbing violently at his face. Miranda tore off the other scarves, frantically unwound the strings of beads from her neck, wrists and ankles, hopping up and down as she tried to walk forward. "What time do you think it is?" she hissed, gathering all her finery in one fist and trying to jam it into her pocket.

"About fifteen minutes past 'we're dead,' " Adam answered.

"Go to your house." Miranda gave him a little push. "Let me handle Daddy till he calms down."

He swerved right back to her side. "Uh-uh. We did this together, we'll face him together. We didn't do anything wrong."

Miranda caught herself biting her nails again. As they crossed the lawn together, she knew her father could see them now. His face was lifted, aimed at them. But his glasses mirrored the light. She couldn't read his expression.

A bird began warbling overhead. It was definitely morning.

Miranda could see his face now. But it was still unreadable. He unfolded his arms and pushed his glasses up.

"Dr. Gates . . . ," Adam began as they approached.

Richard held up his hand. He began nodding to himself as if an invisible voice were telling him things. "Well, well, well. Good morning, Adam. If that's really your name. You and my daughter, who is a minor child, are really up early this morning."

Miranda remembered he'd been drinking last night and might be less rational than usual. "Daddy—"

His hand shot out toward her, palm up, so suddenly

211

she flinched. "Give me that stuff!" he shouted. "It belongs to my mother!"

She realized he was talking about the scarves and beads trailing out of her pocket. She dug them out meekly, and he snatched them, stuffing them into his own pocket. Then he turned back to Adam. "What the hell kind of game were you making her play?"

Adam stepped forward, turning his body as if to screen Miranda. "No, man! It's not anything like that. Just let us come in and I'll explain to you—"

Now Richard's finger shot out, pointing at Adam. "Look how red his face is!" he said to Miranda.

"His face isn't red!" Miranda was getting angry. "He has lipstick on it!"

"Don't help me," Adam said to her.

"It isn't bad enough you molest her! You make her paint her face like a whore and put on my mother's jewelry. I don't even want to know what the scarves were for!"

"You've got a sick mind, man," Adam said.

The two men stepped closer, as if they had heard a signal. Miranda's father's hand began shuttling frantically back and forth between his heart and the space between them. "Tell me what it was really about, Adam. Was it because she was the only thing I had left that you hadn't taken from me?"

212

Adam was gesturing, too, holding both hands out palm up, like a beggar. "Everything that happens in the world isn't about you!"

"You think I'm too weak to retaliate, right? You think you have me all sized up!"

"You're like . . . dreaming or something!"

"I've had to contend with people like you all my life. . . . "

"Why don't you let me tell you what we were doing!"

"Would that be part of the fun? Standing here in my face telling me? I know what! Let's fix it so you can tell the whole story to a magistrate!"

"You can't scare me! I'm not scared of you because I didn't do anything wrong!"

"You will be scared of me before this is over, son. Believe me."

"Don't call me son. I'll tell you what this is really about. It's about me inheriting this land." Adam pointed to the ground. "Now you're just looking for a way—"

Richard pulled a string of Lila's beads from his pocket and waved them in Adam's face. "If I wanted the land, I'd offer you these! It worked before!"

"Daddy!" Miranda didn't think she'd ever felt so angry in her life. It was like a paralysis.

Richard turned his cold, raging eyes on her. "You get in the house and wash your face! I haven't decided what I'm going to do with you!"

Adam stepped between them. "You leave her alone!"

"She's my daughter, dammit! That's one thing you're not taking away from me!"

Adam's hands came up again. "Look, I don't want to take anything—"

"Get out of here!" Richard tapped Adam's chest lightly. "Get off my property!"

"It isn't your property!"

Richard flinched as if Adam had hit him. A shudder ran through his body. He stepped forward, his right hand slowly rising.

Adam took a step backward. A wild look came into his eyes. "Don't," he whispered.

Miranda grabbed her father's arm. "Don't you dare hit him!"

His body turned in the direction it was pulled in, which aimed the slapping hand at Miranda's face. "I told you to get in the house!" he shrieked.

There was a sound from Adam that could only be called a growl. He threw himself on Richard. Miranda stepped back, afraid they would both fall on her. Richard crumpled and Adam jumped on top, drew a fist back and smashed it into Richard's mouth. "Don't you ever hit her!" he screamed, although his face looked as if he was crying. "You hear me?"

Miranda grabbed Adam and dragged him off.

Richard pulled himself up on his elbows. His mouth was bleeding, but his eyes looked almost gleeful.

"I'm sorry," Adam said, weeping openly. "You looked like—"

Miranda let go of Adam and went to her father. "Are you okay?" she asked.

"I'm sorry, Dr. Gates. I'm sorry," Adam chanted, wiping his face on his T-shirt. "We both went crazy."

Richard let Miranda pull him to his feet. He was sort of smiling. He looked at Adam a few seconds, turned without a word and went into the house, closing the door.

"Miranda, I'm sorry!" Adam said. "He was going to hit you!"

"I don't think so." She looked nervously at the house. "He never hit me before."

"I can't stand to see—"

"I know, but you shouldn't have . . ."

The door opened again. Richard was holding a wet paper towel to his mouth. "I called 911," he reported. "I said I didn't need an ambulance, but they're sending a cruiser out here." He looked at Miranda. "None of my teeth are loose, thank god."

Adam had turned white. "Dr. Gates, when they get here you have to tell them—"

"I'll tell them what happened," Richard said. The door closed again.

Adam looked at Miranda. His eyes were wide, as if he were seeing or remembering something terrible. His whole body shook. He took off running to his own house.

Miranda stared after him. She sat down in the grass. In the east, a lovely seashell pink was seeping into the sky. The grackles were up, whistling and perching at the feeder.

"Shut up," Miranda said to them.

The sky was red and flaming when the cruiser pulled up. Miranda heard the crunch of gravel, saw the flashes out of the corner of her eye. She still didn't move. It was as if something had drained from her. If they arrested Adam, they could find out he was a fugitive from the State of Tennessee.

She heard the front door opening and closing and her father's voice, speaking quietly and rapidly, telling his story. There seemed to be a male voice and a female voice interrupting with questions. "He's over there right now?" the male voice asked clearly. More inaudible conversation and the front door closed again.

The policewoman came around the side of the house and walked up to Miranda. She had a friendly face and a pear-shaped figure that didn't look good in a police uniform. Her black hair was pulled into a long ponytail that hung down her back, and she had straight bangs across her forehead like a little girl. "Are you Miranda?" she asked.

"Yes." Miranda stared at the empty bird feeders. One of the grackles was staring back.

"Did you see what happened?" Since Miranda refused to look up, the officer had to kneel in the grass to look her in the eye. She had freckles on her nose.

"My father and my . . . boyfriend . . . got in a fight."

"Your boyfriend lives in that little house?"

"He did. He used to work for my grandmother. We were visiting her and she died. And Adam inherited this property. So now this is all his, and he's letting us stay."

"I see. So there's a lot of crosscurrents going on here?"

Miranda noticed that the officer was talking to her like an adult. But maybe it was a trick, like good cop, bad cop. Maybe this cop's partner was bashing in Adam's head right now.

"Yeah . . . ," Miranda said, trying to choose her words carefully. "But the main thing is Adam and I were out . . . walking in the marsh last night and we got back late and Daddy thought—"

"So a fight broke out."

"Yes."

The officer readjusted her knees as if the ground

wasn't too comfortable. "Well, Miranda, you're a fairly important witness. Because if your father says one thing and Adam says another, we're going to give a lot of weight to what *you* say."

"Yes." Not only was Adam doomed, but Miranda would be the last nail in his coffin.

"Your father says the three of you were arguing and Adam pushed him to the ground and punched him in the mouth with a closed fist."

"That's most of it."

"What's the rest?"

"My father looked like he was going after me. He had his hand raised like this, first to Adam and then to me."

"Does he ever do that? Slap you?"

"No. But Adam didn't know that. He was trying to help me." Miranda wanted to go on and explain that Adam got beat up by his father, but maybe that was a secret Adam didn't want her to tell.

"Did your father strike or touch Adam at any time during the confrontation?"

"He tapped him once, like this, but that's it." Miranda touched the officer lightly on the arm. "Only in the chest."

"Just a tap like that? No harder?"

Miranda felt like Judas Iscariot. "No."

The officer patted Miranda and stood up. "Okay, Miranda, that's what I needed to know."

Miranda stood up and followed her around to the front of the house. At the same time, Adam and the other officer, a tall black man, were walking over from his house. At least he didn't have the cuffs on yet.

Adam and Miranda gave each other edgy looks.

"He admits to it, says he'll apologize if Dr. Gates agrees not to press charges. His mouth didn't look that bad. I don't think . . ."

"Right," said the female officer. She sprinted up the steps and rang the bell. "Maybe we can . . ."

The door opened. Richard came out on the porch. There was a slight red mark under his lower lip. No blood. "Well?"

"Adam would like to apologize to you," the male officer said.

Adam looked up at Miranda's father, eyes frankly pleading. "Dr. Gates, I'm really sorry. I lost my temper and it was a big mistake. You know, we've all had a lot of—"

"Okay, he apologized," Richard interrupted. "Now what?"

The policeman sighed. "You still want to press charges?"

"Damn right I do! He punched me in the mouth. That's a crime, isn't it?"

"Yes, it is, but seeing that there's been all this upset in your family—"

"He's not my family! He's got nothing to do with my family!"

"Dr. Gates, please." Adam's voice had a little edge of terror. "I did a very bad thing and I'll never do it again, I promise you, but—"

"I don't understand why I'm being made to listen to this," Richard said. "Is this your policy when somebody's assaulted? You try to have the parties shake hands and make up? Is that the law in Florida?"

"Daddy—" Miranda began.

"Don't waste your breath," Adam said. "He's out to screw me because he knows he can."

The male officer turned to Adam. "Let's watch the language. This man has the right to press charges if he wants to. You had a choice whether to hit him or not, and you made that choice. This is the consequence."

"I know," Adam said.

Out came the handcuffs. Adam's body jerked in an odd way as if his feet had tried to run but the rest of him held back. "We have to do this, Adam, for your protection and ours," the policeman was saying smoothly. Adam had already turned his back and put his hands together. He knew about this.

"You have the right to remain silent. . . ."

Miranda ran up the steps, past her father, into the house. She wasn't going to watch them take him away.

A while later there was a knock on Miranda's door. She ignored it, but Richard came in anyway. "Are you ready to talk to me?" he said.

It was such a stupid opening, Miranda didn't even know how to answer.

"I did the right thing," he said. "I know you like him, but he's got a dangerous temper. Do you want to get mixed up with a guy who can lose it that easily?"

"He was defending me."

"Come on, Miranda. I know he's got you all manipulated and confused, but—"

"Daddy. You don't know anything."

"Miranda, come on. All we have left is each other."

Miranda sat up. "How much clearer do I have to say it, Dad? I'm not on your side. You've been wrong about . . . practically everything since we came to Florida. You're wrong about Grandma's land and you're wrong about Adam, and I'm just starting to realize you're all wrong about me, too. But, hey, you're winning, so what do you care? You've got your blackmail thing now, why don't you call Skip and tell him? Adam will do anything you say to get out of jail, I'm sure. You're in control, Dad. Open a six-pack and celebrate."

"Hey, you—"

"But the thing is, Daddy, you're not catching the

other side of it. Have you noticed it's getting very quiet around here? You're losing everybody, one by one. Your own mom couldn't trust you . . . and you obviously did something to make Ariel run away. Guess who's next? I've been killing myself trying to stay loyal to you, but you make it really, really hard."

"You don't—"

"You know who you'll end up with? Skip Wilson. And after he gets the property, he might dump you. You bet on all the wrong stuff and you think you won, but you lost and you made me lose, too." Miranda turned away from him and looked out the window.

After a long pause she heard the door quietly close.

fifteen

The Turtle Island Law Center looked like a converted drugstore. It stood between Davis Lighting and Fixtures and Turk's Barber Shop. Across the street, beside the post office, was Wilson Development Corporation.

The Law Center's glass door was crowded with stenciled information. TURTLE ISLAND SHERIFF'S DEPARTMENT. BUREAU OF MOTOR VEHICLES, AUTO REGISTRATION, FISHING LICENSES, HOMESTEAD EXEMPTIONS, MONDAY– FRIDAY 10 AM–5 PM. NO PET'S BICYCLES BEYOND THIS DOOR.

It would have made Miranda laugh if she hadn't been so scared. She pushed the heavy glass door open. A black policewoman with a fountain of braids sat behind a high counter in the lobby. Two male officers were drinking coffee at a dinette table off to the side. There were vending machines and several pay phones. A black magnetic board explained where various county services could be found. Detention—Adam—was here on the first floor.

"May I help you?" the policewoman asked. Both the other officers looked up as if girls Miranda's age rarely came into this building.

"I want to visit one of your prisoners," Miranda said. She spoke loudly so that even if they didn't let her see Adam, her voice might carry and he'd know she'd come.

"We've only got one," she replied. "How old are you, honey?"

"I'm fifteen," Miranda said. "But I really want to see him. He's my boyfriend." She hoped at least one of these three people would have a heart and feel sorry for them.

The policewoman looked over Miranda's head at the two others. "He's just a kid himself," she said, as if asking for permission to bend the rules.

"It's domestic, isn't it?" one of them asked. Miranda turned to face a pair of concerned brown eyes. This officer wore a wedding ring. "Did he hit you?"

"No," Miranda said. "He hit my father."

"Does your father know you're here?"

"Yes."

This made them all shoot telepathic glances around, which Miranda couldn't interpret. The brown-eyed officer stood and stretched. "I'll take her back for a second." He started walking toward a hallway.

Miranda hurried after him, smiling at the woman, who she felt had started the ball rolling for her.

"Your friend is pretty bummed out," Miranda's escort told her. He was so tall, she had to trot to keep up with him. "He's one of those people that just wilt in a lockup. So if he doesn't talk to you . . . don't take it personally. He hasn't said a word to us, either."

"I think he'll talk to me," Miranda said, hearing fear in her voice.

They came to the end of a corridor. There was a sort of conference table and a lot of filing cabinets and, at the very back of the room, a single barred cell right out of Mayberry. It was dark and shadowy. Miranda could make out a cot, a sink and a toilet, but not Adam. The air was thick with the smell of Lysol. She moved closer, squinting.

"Don't approach the cell." The officer corralled her gently with his arm. "Stand right there and I'll go back to the hallway so you can have some privacy. But I have to watch you because I definitely don't want you to get close enough to touch him or hand him anything."

Miranda realized he meant a weapon. They didn't even have metal detectors in the building. "Okay."

"Five minutes." He winked at her and then raised his voice to the jovial tone nurses use on hospital patients. "You have a guest, Mr. Fitzgerald. If a nice-looking girl like her came to see me, I wouldn't sit in the corner sulking!" The officer backed away, watching Miranda.

It was weird, having people be nice to you and not trust you at the same time. Miranda turned her attention to the cell. As her eyes adjusted, she could see Adam, sitting on the floor in the corner, wedged in like a cockroach. He didn't look up at her.

Miranda wanted to come forward, but that might blow it. She stood on tiptoe, as if that brought her closer to him. "Adam? It's me."

A weird, hoarse voice threaded through the darkness. "What are you doing here?"

"What am I doing here? I came to see you!"

"I don't want you to," the darkness croaked.

"Adam, are you okay?"

A horrible laugh echoed off the walls.

Miranda took a deep breath. She hadn't realized anyone could slide into a depression so quickly. "Well, I mean, I know you're not okay, but—"

"Go away. I mean it. You can't help me."

Miranda was torn between pity and being pissed off. "Adam, it's me. I'm your friend. Get up and come over here where I can see you!"

Silence.

"Adam, we only have a few minutes."

Silence.

Miranda remembered the panicked cat under the porch. Still, she could hardly sing "Over the Rainbow." But maybe a softer attitude would help. "This is a whole lot worse for you than I can imagine, isn't it?"

"Yeah." A flicker of Adam's normal voice. "Yeah."

Miranda lowered her voice. "It looks like they don't have computers, so . . ."

"Shhh. I know. But down the road . . . I have a hearing scheduled for Friday. That's when the judge gets back from fishing or something."

"Have you called a lawyer?"

"Not yet." The shadow shifted around.

"Not yet! What are you waiting for? Did you say anything to them? Don't you know . . . ?"

"I know. . . ."

"Adam, you can't just be depressed and drift along here. Call the guy who handled the will. He was nice."

"He's not a criminal lawyer. I think they give you a public defender if—"

"You don't need that! You can afford any kind of lawyer you want! Adam, what's wrong with you?"

"I just . . ." He stopped and took a sudden deep breath, as if the air were running out in there. "What's your father doing?"

"Nothing. When I left the house, he was sitting at the

kitchen table, staring into space. I think, with Ariel and everything, he's pretty confused."

"So he and Skip aren't . . . following up on anything?"

"No. I mean, I don't know for sure what Skip might do on his own, but . . ."

"Do you know what Lila told me?"

Miranda glanced at the hallway. The officer was talking to another officer, not watching them. "What?"

"She warned me something like this was going to happen. She said I would have to endure a very hard test." His voice rose, almost a sob. "She wasn't kidding."

"When did she say all this?"

"In our ceremony. She was right in front of me with her hair down like . . . like it looked in the hospital. She said I should remember that she had trusted me to hold on to the land no matter what and that I shouldn't be afraid because if I just held my ground, I'd be okay. So that's what I'm trying . . ." He coughed, the way boys do when they don't want to cry.

Out in the hall, the policeman glanced at his watch and looked at Miranda.

"Adam, they're going to make me go. I love you!"

More coughing. "You too," he choked out.

Miranda felt a large, warm hand on her shoulder. "I'm going to have to cut you off now. We were bending the rules to do this much."

"Okay." Miranda backed away, listening to the whispery echo of Adam trying to control his breathing. If one night in this relatively benign lockup had done this to him, what would a real prison do? And if they knew his record, that might happen.

I hate my father. The thought surfaced, complete in her brain. Miranda knew that if her father went through with this and hurt Adam, she would never forgive him as long as she lived. She'd be like Lila. Cut him off completely. Her heart wouldn't give her a choice.

"Take care of yourself, honey!" the policewoman at the desk called as Miranda pushed open the heavy door. There was a rush of outdoor sounds. The trees were full of birds. If only Adam could hear them.

Trudging home, Miranda passed the Rexall and remembered her photos. She stumbled into the cool, waxy-smelling shadows of the store, hardly noticing Lindsay Baker's malicious smile. "Well, is it true?" Lindsay called out.

Miranda was fumbling in her purse for the stubs. "Is what true?"

Lindsay cracked her bubble gum. "About Adam getting busted and hauled off in a police car."

Miranda felt her face get hot. Lindsay was talking

loudly on purpose. The only other customer in the store, a tall, thin woman, looked up with interest. "I'm here for my pictures," Miranda said. "It's Gates. *G-A-T-E-S.*"

Lindsay continued to smile as she turned to consult her files. "I told you, didn't I? What he was like? I heard the charge was assault. I always thought he was like . . . violent under the surface."

Miranda faked a yawn.

"Who'd he hit? I heard it was a big fistfight with your father. Was Adam messing with your stepmother? I heard she left town."

Miranda controlled her rage by shuddering. "Can't you find the envelopes? It looks like you only have about a dozen there, and five of them are mine!"

Lindsay laughed. "Yeah. Here you go. Hey, I'm sorry if I'm embarrassing you. This is a small island. People talk."

Miranda looked at Lindsay, letting her see she was not afraid to stare right into her eyes. Then she wrote out a check, crumpled it into a tiny ball and tossed it over the counter.

When Miranda got home it was almost lunchtime. Her father had moved from the kitchen table to the picnic table in the backyard. He stared at an empty bird feeder that swung slightly as if something had just flown away.

The kitchen was spotless, so either he hadn't had anything to eat or had cleaned up after himself carefully.

I've got to do something, Miranda thought. *Everything's a mess and there's no one to fix it but me.*

She walked slowly into the yard. Richard looked up at her almost fearfully.

"After I visited Adam I picked up my pictures," Miranda said. "Do you want to look at them with me?"

Richard looked wary. "Why would we want to do that? Probably every picture in there will make us feel bad or remember something sad."

Miranda sat down on the bench next to him. "I think the biggest problem with you and me is that we think if you don't look at something, it isn't there."

Richard's look had turned to a kind of stare. "You've changed so much."

Miranda broke the seal on the envelope. "How?"

He swallowed hard. "You're starting to remind me of your mother."

Miranda laid out the photos one by one, like a fortune-teller turning cards. The whole story was there. Black-and-white pictures of the drive to Florida, the interior of the car looking claustrophobic, a storm gathering, Richard and Ariel squabbling.

Richard looked at these with no expression, but he

inhaled sharply at the last shot on the black-and-white rolls. The bridge to Turtle Island. "The minute I saw this place again, I felt like something inside me was coming apart," he said.

"Me too," Miranda said.

Suddenly, just like in the *Wizard of Oz,* there was color. The images sprang to life: the rising sun glinting on Lila's iridescent wind chimes, wind rippling the saw grass, waterbirds wheeling in the sky.

"I haven't even taken a walk in the marsh since I got here," Richard said. "I think I'm afraid to."

Miranda continued to present pictures without comment. There was Adam, raising his arms to pray. "He's really suffering in there," Miranda said. "Brace yourself, I think Lila's the next shot."

And she was—strolling down the marsh trail, singing. Lifting her African storyteller's stick with a flourish. Cheeks flushed, eyes sparkling, wisps of hair escaping their pins and floating on the wind. Alive.

Richard covered his eyes with one hand, just for a second, then stared at the picture hard. "Keep going," he said.

But Miranda put the pictures back in the envelope. "Let's take a walk in the marsh instead," she said. "And look at the real thing."

232

The birds were relatively quiet, the air hot and humid. A few orange dragonflies buzzed low to the ground. Miranda and her father walked for several minutes without speaking. Then Richard said, "I know I've been wrong about a lot of things."

"Adam," Miranda said. "You've been wrong about him, and what you did to him was vindictive. It wasn't like you at all."

He kept his eyes on the ground. "I just wanted to get him out of the way. That's what I do with disturbing things, Miranda. I just try to push them out of the way."

Something splashed in the canal behind them. They turned to see an anhinga bob up with a silver fish in its beak.

"Me too," Miranda said. "Was that why you wanted to make that deal with Skip, Dad? Is this marsh one of the disturbing things you wanted to get out of the way?"

"There's a place I'd like to show you," he said.

After a few more minutes Miranda realized where they were going, and her heart began to pound. They rounded the bend that was still familiar to her in the daylight, and Richard stopped, looking at the hill, the four pine trees with their fronds fluttering like flags.

Miranda's voice was faint with wonder. "Why is this place special to you?"

He rested a hand on her shoulder. "I used to sit on that hill with your mother. That was the place where I proposed."

An urge to cry swept over Miranda like a gust of wind. She closed her eyes tightly, squeezing out tears. She felt her father take her hand.

"What can I do to help you?" he asked softly.

"Let's go sit there," Miranda choked out. "Let's sit on that hill and talk about my mother. I have questions I've been wanting to ask you for years."

Now his voice was strangled. "Okay."

They climbed the hill together.

CHAPTER

sixteen

Just as they reached the backyard, Miranda and her father heard the crunch of gravel. Miranda knew somehow it was Skip Wilson's car. Her father let go of her hand and quickened his pace as he rounded the house. Miranda trotted to keep up.

Skip was on the porch, knocking on the front door.

"Hi." Richard's voice was neutral.

Skip broke into a huge grin and vaulted off the porch, not bothering with steps. "There you are, you boy genius! You master manipulator! I thought all that shrink training was a waste of time, but now I've seen the light."

Richard folded his arms. "What are you talking about?"

"How'd you do it?" Skip was now playfully boxing with Richard, almost doing a little dance around him.

Richard stepped back. "How'd I do what?"

"How'd you pull off the coup of the century? You've got the enemy all locked up, right across the street from my office. Just waiting for us to come down with the proper paperwork, which I took the liberty of drawing up this morning. We'll swap him his freedom for the land. This is historic, man! It's like a reenactment!"

Richard just stared at him. As if, Miranda thought, he were seeing his friend for the first time.

"How'd you do it is what I want to know," Skip said. "I mean you saved us the detective fee. How'd you get him to hit you like that? Did you use a secret shrink trick? Push his buttons?"

"I'm going in the house," Miranda said.

"No," said Richard. "Stay here."

"Anyway, we can transfer the deed right there—one-stop shopping—and you can drop the charges on him—"

"I'm dropping the charges anyway," Richard said.

"And we can head over to the Snapping Turtle for a little— What'd you say?"

"I'm going downtown right now to drop the charges. I should never have pressed charges in the first place."

Skip grabbed Richard's shoulders. "Wait. Wait.

You're freaking out." He turned to Miranda. "You've been working on him, haven't you?"

"I'm a person in my own right, Skip." Richard stepped back again, letting Skip's hands slide off. "Every time I make a decision, it doesn't mean somebody influenced me."

Skip's eyes flashed at Miranda. "You worked on him to get your boyfriend out of jail, didn't you? Where's your loyalty, Miranda? Don't you know this guy is practically stealing from your father?"

"Talk to me, Skip." Richard raised his voice slightly. "Look at me. I want you to understand. I've been mentally screwed up since we came back here. It was like I crossed the bridge and I was fifteen again. And you were my hero—"

"Listen, Rich—"

"But you're not. You haven't been for a long time. I don't blame you for being the way you are. You can't help it. But I never should have made that stupid agreement with you in the first place. It left my mother no choice but to take my inheritance away from me, and I think it drove my wife away and it damn near alienated me from my only daughter."

"If you would just—"

"And do you know why? Because I just wanted to be a kid again and drink beer and ride in back of a pickup truck. I wanted to forget all my responsibilities and problems. I wanted to plow under this whole piece of land because every time I see it, all I can think of is Jasmine. . . . " Richard choked, looking away.

"You're telling yourself a story, man. You think too much. That's always been your trouble."

Richard composed himself, straightened his spine. "And you don't think enough!"

The two men stared at each other. Richard's face was calm, but Skip's eyes were agitated. "Rich, you can't do this to me. This piece of land is the key to everything I've been trying to do for the past ten years. I was counting on you!"

Richard folded his arms. "Sorry."

Skip's breathing quickened. "You're a wuss, Richard! You're caving in to a bunch of women and tree-huggers! Can't you be a man?"

"This discusson is over," Richard said. "I have to get downtown."

Skip looked from Miranda to her father, then back to Miranda. His blue eyes blazed. "Okay. Great. Fine. But don't consider me your friend anymore."

"I don't."

Skip strode to his car, turned and strode back to them. "You're really doing me a favor, Rich! This stupid town has been holding me back for years! Do you know what a guy like me could do in Hilton Head? Or

Orlando? Jesus! Like this stinking little swamp is so great!" He marched back to the car, jerked the door open and poked in one leg. He looked like a stork or a spider. "Thank you, Richard! Thank you very, very much! I've been marooned on this island long enough. I'm going out and join the twentieth century!" He slid into the seat hard, accidentally honking the horn with his belt buckle.

"You better hurry," Richard said quietly. "The twentieth century is almost over."

Skip scowled, slammed the car door, shifted and sprayed gravel. Long after he was gone, the dust from his wheels hung in the air.

While Adam helped Richard load the car, Miranda pivoted around the backyard, taking pictures. She kept worrying she would miss something. The grackles were on the feeder as usual, one of them sorting Wild Bird Mix with fierce jabs of his beak, shoving the undesirable thistle seed on the ground to get at the cracked corn. "If I ever decide to believe in spirit guides, I'm going to choose you," she told the grackle, lining him up in her viewfinder. He puffed into a ridiculous shape, as if to ruin her picture on purpose.

Miranda came around the front, taking a sneaky shot

of Adam in his black tank top, lifting a heavy box. Wesa was sleeping on the front porch. Miranda picked him up and kissed him, then took several shots of him settling back down into his nap. When she looked at Adam again, he was staring at her urgently. Her stomach tightened. In a few minutes they'd be leaving.

"I'm going in the house for a minute," Richard said. "Make sure we haven't forgotten anything."

They waited until he was inside the house. Then Miranda ran down the porch steps, stopping just short of a collision with Adam, who moved just as fast. "He did that on purpose so we could say good-bye," Miranda said.

Adam took another step. Their bodies brushed. Miranda had never really felt shy with him before, but she did now. "I wish we could stay the rest of the summer, but . . ."

"I know. Your dad needs to regroup. I meant what I said, though. You guys can come down here and stay anytime you want. I don't want your father to feel he has to leave this place behind."

"I don't think he will," Miranda said. "I don't think he can."

"And I don't want you to leave me behind." He put his hands on her arms, which Miranda realized she had crossed over her heart.

"Not after all we've been through," Miranda said, looking down at the grass.

"You're fifteen. You're going a thousand miles away to a big-city high school. I can't ask you not to go on dates and stuff."

Miranda looked up into his eyes. "Adam, we're special. I know it as much as you do. I could go off and marry some guy and have six children and it wouldn't change us."

He laughed. "Don't do that, though."

"I'll be back here. Whether Daddy comes or not. I'll always come back here to you. I . . . love you."

His shoulders, which had been tense, relaxed. "I love you, too. Can I give you something, Miranda?"

Miranda was afraid it would be a ring. Not that she would mind, but it would be hard to explain to her father that you could make a commitment at fifteen and know it would be right for the rest of your life.

Adam fished in his pocket and pulled out a rock. A plain chunk of limestone.

Miranda laughed with relief. "From the marsh?"

"Yeah. I want you to have a piece of it to hold wherever you are. I want you to get real confused about whether it's me or the marsh you love. I know one of us can make you come back."

"Better make sure." Miranda tucked the rock in her

pocket and tipped her head back. "Give me a little piece of you, too."

His mouth was as warm as his hands.

Neither of them spoke for the first few miles. It was Richard who broke the silence. "Are those Mom's beads?"

Miranda looked down at her wrist, where she had roped a strand of Lila's iridescent pink beads. "Yeah. It turns out I kind of like some of these silly things."

He looked over at her. "You remind me more and more of your mother."

Miranda smiled. "I'm like both of you, Dad. And a little like Lila. And one part that's just me and nobody else."

Richard turned back to face the road. "Do you think I would make a complete fool of myself if I called Ariel?"

"What if you do?" Miranda said. "It's worth a try. Anyway, I miss her."

"Me too. So tell me this. Do I want to know how serious you are about Adam?"

Miranda laughed. "I don't think you do."

He smiled. "You're right. Anyway, worst-case scenario, you'll marry him and bring the property back into the family."

Miranda laughed and took a picture of her father's smile. Then she leaned out the window with her camera, framing the thick, colorful hammocks of slash pine, cypress and red maple, waiting for just the right composition, closing the shutter, stopping time, feeling her power.

About the Author

JOYCE SWEENEY was born in Dayton, Ohio. She graduated with honors from Wright State University. Her first book, *Center Line,* won the first annual Delacorte Press Prize for an Outstanding First Young Adult Novel. Her most recent book for Delacorte Press is *Free Fall.* She also teaches workshops in creative writing and is active in the Book Group of South Florida. She lives in Coral Springs, Florida, with her husband, Jay, and cat, Macoco.

Praise for Joyce Sweeney's books

Free Fall

AN ALA QUICK PICK FOR YOUNG ADULTS
☆ "Four high school boys are lost for twenty-four hours in an underground cave in this suspenseful adventure story. . . . Lean and skillfully wrought, this novel hooks the reader and doesn't let go."

—*Publishers Weekly,* Starred

"Crackles with tension to the last breathless moment of the story. Young adults will devour this book in one voracious gulp."

—*Children's Book Review Magazine*

"Sweeney mixes excitement with finely crafted characters and credible psychological underpinnings to deliver a powerful YA novel."

—*Booklist*

Shadow

An ALA Best Book for Young Adults

An ALA Quick Pick for Young Adults

☆ "Characters are realistically drawn, and the plot is riveting."

—*School Library Journal,* Starred

☆ "This page-turner is a psychic novel built around realistic feelings, emotions, hates, fears, and love. . . . This cover is a winner, and so is the novel it encloses."

—*Voice of Youth Advocates,* Starred